Mr. Robot and Philosophy

Popular Culture and Philosophy® Series Editor: George A. Reisch

For full details of all Popular Culture and Philosophy® books, visit www.opencourtbooks.com.

Popular Culture and Philosophy®

Mr. Robot and Philosophy

Beyond Good and Evil Corp

EDITED BY

RICHARD GREENE AND
RACHEL ROBISON-GREENE

OPEN COURT
Chicago

Volume 109 in the series, Popular Culture and Philosophy®, edited by George A. Reisch

To find out more about Open Court books, visit our website at www.opencourtbooks.com.

Open Court Publishing Company is a division of Carus Publishing Company, dba Cricket Media.

Printed and bound in the United States of America.

Printed and bound in the United States of America.

Mr. Robot and Philosophy: Beyond Good and Evil Corp

ISBN: 978-0-8126-9961-6

Library of Congress Control Number: 2017939160

This book is also available as an e-book.

For Becca Robison
(Because of how much she loves robots!)

If you wrestle with monsters, take care you don't become a monster yourself. Keep staring into the abyss and the abyss will stare right back into you.

—FRIEDRICH NIETZSCHE, *Beyond Good and Evil:*
Prelude to a Philosophy of the Future

Contents

Contents

Thanks

Working on this project has been a pleasure, in no small part because of the many fine folks who have assisted us along the way. In particular, a debt of gratitude is owed to David Ramsay Steele and George Reisch at Open Court, the contributors to this volume, and our respective academic departments at UMass Amherst and Weber State University.

Finally, we'd like to thank those family members, students, friends, and colleagues with whom we've had fruitful and rewarding conversations on various aspects of all things *Mr. Robot* as it relates to philosophical themes.

Real, This Book?

Hello, friend. I'm going to talk to you about something, but I'm not sure that it's real. For that matter, I'm not even sure that you are real.

It's this book. It claims to be an irresistibly fascinating book that explores all sorts of fantastic philosophical themes that can be found in some television show called *Mr. Robot*.

In this show there is an Evil Corporation and they pretty much control the whole kingdom of bullshit. Mr. Robot and some plucky kids that kinda remind me of the Scooby gang on *Scooby Doo*, or maybe that other Scooby gang on *Buffy the Vampire Slayer*, attack this Evil Corporation by hacking into its computers and bring it to its knees.

The group that attacks Evil Corporation calls itself "fsociety," which is pretty funny, if you think about it. It all seems kinda fun-loving and cool until you start to delve a little deeper. I mean, if fsociety brings down society, by crippling its financial institutions, what else happens? What are the philosophical implications of this kind of thing? What will replace the Evil Corporation? Will there ever be order again? Was there ever order in the first place?

And you gotta ask, "Why did those kids do it?" It seems like it might have been based on some political ideology, but on closer inspection it might have just been an act of revenge. After all, Evil Corp killed Elliot's and Darlene's Dad (Elliot and Darlene are the leaders of fsociety). Or did they? Are either of these reasons justified? Does justification even matter in circumstances such as these?

And what about hacking? Is hacking ever okay? What if it's to catch someone really bad like a pedophile or a drug dealer? Man, that's a lot of questions! I sure hope that this book is real, because I need answers to these questions and all the other ones that the philosophers in this book are tackling.

I should stop talking now because I've probably already said too much. Also, if I'm right about reality being such a mystery, you probably don't even know whether I'm real. I guess the only way we're gonna get to know what we should and shouldn't believe is to dive into this book (if it exists).

I

We're All Living in Each Other's Paranoia

1
The Deed of F'ing Society

JAMES ROCHA

Hello Reader.

"Hello Reader"? That's lame. I'm copying the show. This is a slippery slope.

Back to you, dear reader. You look stressed. This is about your debt, isn't it?

Don't worry. I'm not reading your mind—just your emails. And chats, and private messages on social media.

Your debt is getting to you—crushing you. It's giving you panic attacks. As Darlene says: "In this day and age, it's sicker not having panic attacks" ("eps2.2_init_1.asec").

So, I understand. It isn't your fault. There's a vast conspiracy out there, bigger than all of us . . . But now I'm getting melodramatic.

The problem is much bigger than you. Responsibility is elusive, exploitation is rampant, free choice masks illusionary options (is Blue Cross or Blue Shield really a free choice?), the coercive institutions that make up our hierarchal, even patriarchal, capitalist society are . . .

Your eyes are glazing over. I'm not helping you by giving philosophical treatises about the limitations on choice within a systematically oppressive society. That won't save you.

Here, let me try this. Give me a second . . .

There. I've deleted all of your debt.

Go ahead: go outside and celebrate. Dance. Sing. Cry. I'll be here when you get back.

Welcome back. How did it feel?

That's the feeling of real freedom. Back when you were shackled by your debt, you thought you had freedom. You were told you had freedom. You were told you were free to choose as you pleased. But it was never real freedom. Your choices were always constricted by society's various controlling influences. Society only gave you a freedom mirage.

Fuck society.

Yes. We agree on that. But how? Propaganda of the deed is how.

The Bug's Only Purpose

Propaganda of the deed is an anarchist notion that refers to spreading propaganda through shocking acts that force people to wake up and take notice.

Don't let anarchism scare you. Anarchism is simply the belief that there can be no justified state. So, anarchists would like to replace the state with a completely new system—maybe one without any hierarchy at all.

But if they do that, what happens to this society?

Fuck this society.

Easier said than done. Our society has problems. We all know that. Donald Trump is our president. Clearly, there are problems. But how do we convince people to leave this society for a new one that leaves hierarchy behind?

You are used to hierarchy. We all say we're against it, but hierarchy makes us feel warm and safe at night. You and I each have our places within the hierarchy. You'd prefer a higher place, but you fear a lower place. I know the feeling of false hope mixed with sincere fear. But, still, your place feels comfortable. As Elliot pointed out, you want to be sedated to maintain that illusion of comfort, "because it is painful not to pretend" ("Eps1.0_hellofriend.mov").

How are we going to convince anyone to leave hierarchy behind when we are all cowards? Not through some boring philosophical lecture on the nature of free choice, that's for sure. Anarchists argue that we need acts that shock people out of their social slumber. That's what Mr. Robot and fsociety are doing.

They're providing the bug: the mistake so big that society has to fundamentally adapt and evolve into something new. That's propaganda of the deed: doing something that forces people to fix society.

But you're worried. Are fsociety's actions justified? Did they go too far? You feel comfortable in your place within the hierarchy. Tearing society apart isn't pretty. But you also want to change the world.

Annihilation Is Always the Answer

Some anarchists believe any deed can be justified if it serves the purpose of the larger cause. Emma Goldman and Alexander Berkman believed in violent propaganda of the deed.

Berkman shot a man. He just went up to one of the richest men in American and shot him. They thought, as Evil Corp CEO Phillip Price says, "A man can change the whole world with a bullet in the right place" ("eps2.1_k3rnel-pan1c.ksd").

According to Goldman, such violent acts are not born out of cruelty, but representative of a "supersensitiveness to the wrong and injustice surrounding them" (*Red Emma Speaks*, p. 257). It's because anarchists see the "conspiracy bigger than all of us," which includes, "the guys that play God without permission" ("eps1.0_hellofriend.mov") (such as Henry Clay Frick—the industrialist who Goldman and Berkman felt was responsible for the deaths of steel workers, and who Berkman shot), that they feel the need to turn to violence.

Propaganda of the deed, in this sense, means doing whatever it takes to bring people's attention to the evil being done in the world, sometimes being done in our names. Elliot's father told him that just by moving sand in his shoe, from the beach to home, he was changing the world ("eps1.4_3xpl0its.wmv"). Yet Elliot realized that it would take many lifetimes to move the beach in that way; he wasn't really making a difference. Most of us don't have the stomach to do what it takes to change the world ("eps1.4_3xpl0its.wmv"). If it takes violent deeds, most of us won't be able to do that.

That's why you've been freaking out. You, especially, don't have the stomach for it. You don't even know if the ends justify violent means. I don't think violence is necessarily justified here either. Fortunately, other anarchists have different views.

Edit Out the Parts We Hate

Not all anarchists believe that the deeds that spark change are morally permitted to be violent. At the other extreme are the pacifist anarchists: the Angelas of the anarchist world.

Consider Mohandas Gandhi, who considered himself an anarchist, but definitely not the violent kind (Peter Marshall, *Demanding the Impossible*, p. 422). While Gandhi rejected the use of violence, he did not support a passive response to injustice: "My creed of non-violence is an extremely active force. It has no room for cowardice or even weakness." Yet, he felt that it's insufficient to simply reason with your opponents: "Reason has to be strengthened by suffering and suffering opens the eyes of understanding." Thus, Gandhi recommended deeds that involved suffering, such as fasting, for the sake of awakening an empathetic understanding from one's opponents. As he put it, "The object always is to evoke the best in him. Self-suffering is an appeal to his better nature, as retaliation is to his baser" ("Resistance to Evil: The Method of Satyagraha").

Even Emma Goldman eventually changed her views on whether violence is a part of anarchism:

> The philosophy of Anarchy is based on harmony, on peace; and it recognizes the right of every individual to life, liberty and development, and opposes all forms of invasion; consequently, the philosophy of Anarchy is an absolute foe to violence, therefore I do not advocate violence.

Goldman still believed that there was a need for anarchists to practice anarchism, get out the message, and set an example that change is possible: "Yet if liberty is ever to bless mankind, it is only when the example set by the few will be followed by the many" ("An Open Letter," pp. 434–35).

For Gandhi and Goldman, positive actions have to be taken in the name of justice to get the message out that another way is possible. Something has to be done. Someone has to be willing to do something. Remember in "eps1.8_m1rr0r1ng.qt" how Angela responds to Terry Colby:

> **TERRY COLBY:** Every fast food joint around the corner delivers diabetes to millions of people. Phillip Morris hands out lung cancer on the hour, every hour. I mean, hell, everyone's destroying the planet beyond the point of no return. Are you going to start taking all of these things so personally?
>
> **ANGELA:** Maybe I will. Maybe someone has to.

The Whole Thing Is a Fall

You're wondering where fsociety fits in. If they are anarchists, and they seem to be, are they the violent kinds like Alexander Berkman? Or are they the pacifist kinds like Gandhi? Closer to the younger Emma Goldman or to the older one?

The destruction of Evil Corp's data certainly isn't self-suffering, as Gandhi recommends. Other people are hurt by fsociety's actions. Along with lost debt records, people lost the records of their mortgages and savings. Credit cards aren't working, and who among us has cash?

While fsociety's actions are not Gandhi's self-suffering, they are not Berkman's violent propaganda of the deed either. fsociety is not killing people, at least not directly. After someone kills Gideon Goddard (CEO of Allsafe Security), Elliot must admit to Darlene, "We're on the other side of something we never signed up for."

To which, Darlene responds, "You thought everything was gonna be hunky-fucking-dory?" ("eps2.2_init_1.asec").

It's a fair and appropriate question. What fsociety did was not going to leave things hunky-fucking-dory. People died because of their actions, but the organization didn't intentionally kill anyone. fsociety was not making their point with weapons of violence, but with a logic bomb ("eps2.3_logic-b0mb.hc.")—that is, malicious programming designed to blow up Evil Corp's financial data.

fsociety's actions directly harmed innocents by destroying data and indirectly harmed innocents in violent ways, including getting people killed. From the perspective of pacifist anarchists, they are counterfeit heroes at best. But that does not mean their views are "bullshit masquerading as insight" ("eps1.0_hellofriend.mov"). There is, after all, a large range of anarchist theories, between Gandhi and Berkman, on how to initiate change.

Dead Puppy Oven

Since this is really a war between the "powerful group of people out there that are secretly running the world" ("eps1.0_hellofriend.mov") and the rest of us, it's fair to use just war theory to further our discussion. In just war theory, there are questions that must be asked before taking an action that harms people, especially innocent people. Here are some of the key questions:

- **Necessity question: Is the action necessary to achieve the objective?**
- **Proportionality question: Is the action's harm proportional to the need to meet the objective? Or, is it the least harmful way to achieve the objective?**
- **Justification question: Does the objective justify the harms caused by the action?**
- **Effectiveness question: Is the action likely to achieve the objective?**

If the action is not necessary, then we do not need to go to the other questions. No need to do an action that harms innocent people if we do not have to. If we could meet the objective while harming fewer innocent people, then we should do that instead. Really, what we need to know is whether the objective is valuable enough to make the action worth it. But, none of this matters if we think we will not succeed: you cannot justify an action through an objective that the action will not meet.

We're treating this issue as if this is a war between the haves and the have-nots—the 1s and 0s—precisely because that's what it is. The objective, as you very well realize, is to find a path to justice, to equality, and out of this conspiracy that's bigger than all of us. And, this is not just rhetorical talk about a TV show. As Darlene points out, "The reasons we wanted to do this, the reasons why we all wanted to do this, are real" ("eps1.8_m1rr0r1ng.qt"). And she doesn't just mean real within the TV show's vantage point: the conspiracy, the men playing God, the war between the 1s and 0s— it's all real. You and I have lived in the Kingdom of Bullshit ("eps1.9_zer0-day.avi.") for all too long.

Given that we want out of Bullshit Kingdom, the necessary deed has to be a very big one. fsociety points out that the people who have been enslaved (you and me) need to be freed ("eps1.9_zer0-day.avi"). And it's going to take a substantial action to knock off our shackles. We don't think it should be a violent action, but certainly the size of the problem makes a significantly large action necessary.

It also needs to be the action that causes the least harm. It would be wonderful if that action could be done while sitting behind a computer, where we could, "watch and enjoy the beautiful carnage that we've all created together as a new society rises from the ashes" ("eps1.9_zer0-day.avi"). But we know from the show that it isn't that simple. Chaos results from Elliot's hacking prowess. Much of the harm is indirect and unintentional, but it is also widespread and definitely affects innocent civilians.

That leaves us with more questions: Is fsociety's action proportional to the objective? Given the need for a large action, is there a large one that diminishes harm instead of augmenting it? Are there less harmful alternatives available?

What are you waiting for? I'm asking you!

I don't know either. These are hard questions that Elliot, Darlene, Romero, Trenton, and Mobley are all trying to answer in their own ways. The easy answers you're asking for just aren't here, friend. You'll have to keep thinking about proportionality as you seek out less harmful alternatives.

Invisible Code of Chaos

What about justification? Does the objective justify fsociety's actions?

Berkman thought justice, equality, and revolutionary change justified violent means. Gandhi disagreed and thought that the means is the end: if your means are violent and unjust, then your end is necessarily the same.

fsociety is somewhere between Berkman and Gandhi. Leon tells Elliot: "Like, existence could be beautiful, or it could be ugly, but that's on you." After Elliot asks which one is for him, Leon tells him to "Dream . . . Sometimes you got to close your eyes and really envision that shit, bro. If you like it, then it's beautiful. If you don't? Then you might as well fade the fuck out right now" ("eps2.2_init_1.asec").

Does the world that fsociety envisions justify taking the action that gets us there?

Yes, I'm really asking you again.

These are hard questions. Philosophy, especially revolutionary philosophy, is not easy. I do not have the solutions for you. I'm just pointing out what's at stake.

The problem is that fsociety rarely tells us what the alternative world looks like. When Trenton accuses Darlene of only being interested in "momentary anarchy," it's clear that she herself is interested in a true sense of freedom, as opposed to the illusion of freedom that is experienced by her father, who "works sixty-hour weeks to determine tax loopholes for a millionaire art dealer," on his way to dying in debt ("eps1.6_v1ew-s0urce.flv"). But she doesn't tell us what true freedom looks like.

Anarchists almost never provide the vision of what ideal society looks like. The next society is not up to today's anarchists to shape and guide. Anarchism means that the members of the next society have the right to determine what their society looks like. Anarchists, then, can only say what it would not look like; anarchist society does not look like a Kingdom of Bullshit.

That makes it very hard to figure out whether serious actions, which include harming innocents, are justified in bringing about a society that only exists in our dreams. Is real freedom, as experienced under anarchism, better than illusionary freedom, as we experience it? It's hard to know since we have never experienced the former.

And the latter is fairly comfortable. Does Elliot ever look happier than when he's drinking a Starbucks Vanilla Latte in "eps1.2_d3bug.mkv"? As Mr. Robot tells us, we choose to turn off reality: "We turned it off, took out the batteries, snacked on a bag of GMOs while we tossed the remnants in the ever-expanding dumpster of the human condition" ("eps1.9_zer0-day.avi"). So maybe we don't even want real freedom. Maybe we're happy with our Instagram and stupid Marvel movies.

I certainly cannot decide for you whether it's justified. You're going to have to dream on it.

The Programmatic Expression of My Will

The last question, then, is whether fsociety's actions will be effective.

You guessed right. I'm not going to answer this one either. Clearly my imaginary reader is ahead of me once again. This is a question for the show to answer.

Or maybe it's a question for you to answer.

If you want to change the world, you'll need your own answers to these questions.

Here's the twist: this was all about you, reader, all along.

You know about the problems. You see them every day. Now you know how to figure out what you can or should do about it.

Did you see it coming?

You can either hack the world ("eps2.3_logic-b0mb.hc.") or keep things on repeat with your "NCISes" and Lexapro ("eps2.0_unm4sk-pt1.tc."). It's up to you.

One last question:

Is the key in the room? ("eps2.9pyth0n-pt1.p7z.")

2
If I Don't Listen to My Imaginary Friend, Why the Fuck Should I Listen to Yours?

S. EVAN KREIDER

A great deal is made of illusion, delusion, imagination, and deception in *Mr. Robot*: Elliot has his imaginary friends and delusional identities, fsociety makes great use of deceptive tactics as well as literal masks, and so forth. These devices work at a variety of levels, both within the context of the show at the level of plot and character interaction, and as a frame through which the audience views the series. Both the casual viewer and the dedicated fan, presumably experiencing more than a few moments of confusion, might well wonder whether this approach truly adds value to the show, or whether the show could simply be more straightforward.

Luckily, we find good company while asking these questions in the philosophers as far back as ancient Greece. So, we might begin to consider these issues ourselves by asking: what would philosophers such as Plato and Aristotle have thought about *Mr. Robot*?

Plato and the Dangers of *Mimesis*

Arstl384:   yo P!

p1t0:   sup

Arstl384:   u c MrR last night?

p1t0:   lol, dont get me started

Arstl384:   umad bro?

p1t0:   wher 2 start . . .

Plato is one of Western civilization's earliest and harshest critics of the arts. This may seem ironic, considering that he himself once aspired to the profession of poet before turning to a career in philosophy. To the ancient Greeks, "poetry" encompasses all narrative art, so it would have included scripted TV shows, if they had had those.

It was Plato's exposure to the great poetry of his day, and his subsequent philosophical analysis of it, that led him to the belief that poetry was extremely dangerous, both morally and intellectually. In order to understand why a former poet would turn against his former love so thoroughly, we must understand a bit about his more general philosophical orientation.

According to Plato, the key to understanding any artistic medium is *mimesis*, a concept generally understood as "imitation," and for Plato specifically, this comes with the negative connotations of fakery, deception, illusion, and imaginings. On this view, art is nothing more than an inadequate copy of real world objects. For example, a painting of a rose is a mere representation of a small part of what the true rose is: it looks somewhat like the rose, but viewed only from one angle, and missing everything else about it such as its smell and feel.

That's bad enough, but it gets worse once we delve into Plato's larger theories about reality, in which he sees the material world around us as a mere imitation of a higher reality of immaterial objects known as the Forms, which are true, perfect examples of reality. That means that art (such as a picture of a rose) is not just an imitation of a reality (a physical rose), but an imitation of an imitation of true reality (the Form of the Rose).

This view leads Plato to claim that there are two major dangers of the arts. First, they are intellectually dangerous. Real knowledge comes from studying real objects, which are the Forms. Studying physical objects, mere imitations of reality, leads to mere belief rather than knowledge. Even worse, studying the arts, mere *imitations of imitations* of reality, leads to nothing more than the hollow exercise of the imagination, lacking wholly in any real knowledge or even adequate belief.

According to Plato, if our goal is true knowledge, we would do best to avoid the arts altogether, and turn our attention directly to the Forms. Even worse, studying the arts is not just intellectually dangerous, but morally dangerous as well, and for largely the same reasons. True moral ideals are to be found by studying the Forms, such as the Form of the Good. Studying limited examples of good in the physical world (like good people or good laws) leads at best to the occasional true belief, but not real knowledge. Studying the arts (such as fictional characters in television shows, who aren't even real good people, much less the highest reality of the Form of the Good) gives no real moral knowledge at all, but mere imaginings and imitations of it. Therefore, Plato thinks that we can only become wise and virtuous people by philosophical contemplation of the Forms, and that those who seek such things through the arts are doomed to ignorance and vice.

Based on this alone, we can already imagine what Plato would have thought about *Mr. Robot*, and at least at first glance, it wouldn't be very good. From the very first lines of the very first episode, we're immediately brought into Elliot's delusion of a fictional friend:

> Hello, friend. "Hello, friend"? That's lame. Maybe I should give you a name. But that's a slippery slope. You're only in my head. We have to remember that. Shit. It's actually happened. I'm talking to an imaginary person. ("eps1.0_hellofriend.mov")

According to Plato's way of thinking, we've already set ourselves up for intellectual and moral failure. Our main character has created an imaginary person to which he can rationalize and justify his behavior, a sort of ethical red flag that suggests that his behavior will be less than rational or virtuous.

Furthermore, this prevents us, the audience, from accurately assessing the events of the series, due to an inherently unreliable narrator. Even within the show's basic framework, neither the protagonist nor the audience have the straightforward factual account that is needed to makes moral sense of the drama.

Elliot also deceives himself and the other characters with whom he interacts by adopting a fake persona to present to the world, by imitating the behavior that he thinks others want to see. An early example of this is the way in which he interacts with his therapist, Krista. When she asks him why he's angry, he seems to respond:

> The world itself's just one big hoax. Spamming each other with our burning commentary of bullshit masquerading as insight. Our social media faking as intimacy . . . We all know why we do this. Not because *Hunger Games* books make us happy. But because we wanna be sedated. Because it's painful not to pretend. ("eps1.0_hellofriend.mov")

However, a moment later, we see that this was all just in his head, said only to his imaginary audience, and not to Krista at all. He understands her desire to help him, but continues to fake his way through their sessions for some time, thereby preventing himself from getting the help that he needs to become a healthier and better person.

Of course, the most obvious example is that is of Mr. Robot himself, a fictitious alternate personality that Elliot has unknowingly created in order to head up fsociety and enact his own plans to take down Evil Corp. This personality is closely based on his father, but is ultimately just a mere imitation of him, capturing some aspects of the real person but not others, as the painting of the rose does the real rose. Just as Plato claims the imaginative, imitative arts in general do, Mr. Robot misrepresents reality to Elliot and misleads him, bringing him into an organization devoted to domestic terrorism without Elliot's fully informed consent.

> **ELLIOT:** Maybe we should stop it, Darlene.
>
> **DARLENE:** Stop what?
>
> **ELLIOT:** The plan. The hack. Everything. Maybe we shouldn't execute it.
>
> **DARLENE:** What? Why? The minute our infected server gets back on the main network, we're set.
>
> **ELLIOT:** It wasn't me. The whole time. Wasn't really me doing all of that.

Elliot believed for most of the first season that he was free to work with fsociety or not, and in choosing to do so, he's allowed an imaginative construct to deceive him, making him responsible for acts and plans that his rational self has not had the opportunity to assess. For Plato, this sort of irrational behavior is the very essence of immorality.

Plato and the Limited Use of the Arts

Arstl384:	SRSLY?
p1t0:	*shrug*
Arstl384:	it cant be all that bad
p1t0:	. . .
Arstl384:	4real? upside?
p1t0:	brb

If that were all Plato had to say on the subject, things would be simple: art = bad. However, even Plato recognizes that there may be something more to the discussion. In *Republic*—a dialogue that many consider to be the definitive statement of Platonic philosophy—Plato spends a great deal of time theorizing about the nature of a perfect society, in which everyone has a function best suited to their abilities. However, to develop those abilities, a proper education is essential. Plato lays out a system of pedagogy in great detail, and although philosophy lies at its pinnacle, even the lowly arts might serve some limited use along the way.

Plato's ideal society includes a class of people who serve as guardians: essentially a military class that protects the society from foreign invaders and enforces the laws within the society. The guardians themselves are subdivided into two sub-classes: the auxiliaries, who are the rank and file military men and women, and the rulers, who are the leaders of the military and rulers of the society as a whole. In order for the rulers to make wise and just laws for society, they themselves must be wise and just, and as discussed above, this ultimately requires philosophical study, especially of the Forms. However, auxiliaries don't require such detailed philosophical knowledge of the Forms. For them, mere true beliefs (that is, the right ideas, even if not fully understood by those who hold them) suffice, and they can learn those true beliefs through other media besides philosophy.

Specifically, Plato argues that the auxiliaries can make do with poetry, as long as that poetry is carefully edited and censored for content by the wise and virtuous rulers. That is, the rulers would take the poems of Homer, Hesiod, and the like, and change them to make sure that they impart good moral lessons, especially those that will promote courage and a general sense of duty towards one's society and fellow citizens. As an example, Homer's *Iliad* (a story of the ancient war between the Greeks and Trojans), shows the hero Achilles refusing to fight simply because he doesn't feel he's getting the right rewards and respect from the king, which then almost causes the Greeks to lose the war.

Plato's rulers would likely change that, to show Achilles putting aside such petty concerns and fighting with his fellow Greeks for the good of all. In this way, poetry, moderated by those with philosophical knowledge, could still serve a practical use in the education of those not themselves ready for philosophy. Plato even goes on to suggest that the rulers might be able to enjoy the original unedited poetry for its aesthetic beauty, having been inoculated by philosophy against poetry's corrupting influences. So perhaps the arts aren't quite as dangerous as they initially seemed, when handled with care.

Fsociety itself seems to take this approach. They believe that they have a higher moral and political message to communicate to the masses that transcends the corrupt laws of contemporary society. Because their activities are illegal, the only way they can communicate this message is through illusion and deception, tales they tell that are not unlike the fictionalized stories of ancient Greek poetry. Their videos, anonymized both electronically and with the use of masks for the speakers, allows them to do this without fear of reprisals, and the masks also make it about the message rather than the person delivering it, so that the focus is on society's problems, and not simply a new cult of personality.

The masks can also be worn by the populace at large, allowing them to feel unified in their anonymity. There's also a point when the masks can, ironically, lead people to see their truer selves and real beliefs, as the masks allow them to be free of the self that they have been playing at all these years. As Elliot himself says: "How do I take off a mask when it stops being a mask? When it's as much a part of me as me?" ("eps2.0_unm4sk-pt1.tc").

As a more extreme example, Elliot's Mr. Robot personality creates a fictional world set in an Eighties-style sitcom to protect him from harsh truths and circumstances long enough for Elliot to cope with the situation. This imaginative world imitates the typical tropes, including a laugh track, and even a cameo from Alf. The point of this, however, is not to shield Elliot from the truth indefinitely, but to allow him to heal his injuries from a savage beating and figure out a way to get free of his position of helplessness at the hands of the guards who are using him for their illegal website. As Mr. Robot tells Elliot: "Well, I'll let you in on a little secret. This was never gonna be permanent. We did always have a destination. After the beating you took, at least they got you to a doctor. You got yourself pretty messed up. If I were alive, I'd want no part of that agony . . . I'm just trying to help you put it all in the rearview as painlessly as possible. Bring 'er in, kiddo. Now that the worst is behind you, it's time we get you back" ("eps2.4_m4ster-s1ave.aes").

Then there's the whole illusion or delusion of the Mr. Robot personality himself. Elliot does eventually see that Mr. Robot is not real, but merely something that Elliot has created in order to help him realize what he truly believed all along. As Darlene points out to him: "Elliot, the reasons we wanted to do this, the reasons why we all wanted to do this, are real. Maybe you don't realize this, but this was your idea. You came up with this. There is a part of you, somewhere deep down inside, that knows this is the right thing to do" ("eps1.8_m1rr0r1ng.qt").

In this way, Elliot served in both roles, that of the rulers, who know the right thing, and the auxiliaries, who are educated about it indirectly through imaginative tales. Elliot uses his split personality to bring himself around to the ideas that he knew were true but wasn't quite ready to take responsibility for, and so gives himself a kind of moral education in the process.

Aristotle and the True Value of the Arts

Arstl384:	lol
p1t0:	wat
Arstl384:	we can do better IMHO
p1t0:	K, bring it
Arstl384:	u got mimesis all wrong
p1t0:	lets C . . .

Aristotle, Plato's most famous pupil, respected his teacher's views a great deal, but did not always agree with them. He took to heart Plato's basic claim that the arts involve *mime-*

sis, and spent a great deal of time elaborating on the issue in *Poetics*, his famous study of the tragic plays of his time.

Aristotle would still be critical of *Mr. Robot* for non-mimesis reasons. For example, he prefers very simple, linear plots with fairly transparent characters, which certainly doesn't sound like this show. However, when it comes to the *mimesis* involved in these plays, Aristotle would say that it's actually a good thing, not a bad one, that can further our intellect and virtue rather than detract from them.

In particular, Aristotle believes that humans are naturally imitative creatures, and that we learn a great deal about ourselves and our societies through imitation. At the simplest level, children learn to speak, walk, and act generally by watching and imitating older people, especially their parents, who in turn try to provide good examples to imitate. Even at morally and politically more sophisticated levels, people learn to be virtuous by imitating the behavior of their betters, and learn how to contribute to society by imitating their leaders. Of course, all this assumes that the people we are imitating are themselves virtuous, which is not always the case, but this is precisely where the arts come in handy.

What the arts do, especially the dramatic arts (in which Aristotle would have included television programs), is to show us examples of people and societies that we can consider for imitation. Moreover, unlike real life, the arts can provide clear commentary about what things we should see as good, and therefore worthy of imitation, or bad, and therefore not. Tragedies are especially good at serving as cautionary tales, as they are designed to show us not only bad people and situations, but also the tragic flaws that exist even in otherwise good people, and how unvirtuous actions that stem from such flaws inevitably lead to a kind of moral retribution—Aristotle's version of karma, one might say. *Mr. Robot* seems like a particularly good example of the sort of thing that Aristotle had in mind.

From this perspective, Aristotle would have no problem with Elliot's invention and use of the Mr. Robot personality. The illusion of another person allows Elliot to ease himself into the very fsociety that he has created. It gives him the temporary safety net of pretending that the real responsibility lies with someone else, at least until the time when he is ready to accept it. Eventually, Elliot does step up and claim responsibility for fsociety, and is ready to move on without the need for Mr. Robot. To date, he has not been entirely successful in this endeavor, but he has at least arrived at the stage where he is ready to make that move, and that's not something he could have done without the crutch of the Mr. Robot personality:

> **ELLIOT:** What are you so afraid will happen if you tell me the truth?
>
> **MR. ROBOT:** Why do you want to know so bad? Why do you even fucking care?
>
> **ELLIOT:** I don't want to be in denial anymore. I just want to accept what I did and move on. ("eps2.5_h4ndshake.sme")

Aristotle would also strongly disagree with Plato's claim that Elliot's imaginary friend is a bad thing. By framing the series with us, the viewer, as a participant in the drama, even a passive one, the show creates a stronger sense of emotional investment in the events of the series. This in turn helps us to take the show's critique of modern society and fsociety's resistance to it more seriously. At the same time, it also provides a safe distance for us to reflect upon these events, since they don't affect us in reality. As fsociety hacks Elliot's employer AllSafe, the masked person on the screen moralizes:

> Corporate greed is a trickle-down desire that reaches even the bottom of the food chain. And for what? Wealth? Power? It's a pathetic fable . . . Those who are complicit, those who aid the tyrants, those who accept the tyranny have no place in the new order. ("eps1.7_wh1ter0se.m4v")

From the safety and comfort of our living rooms, we can think about this message objectively, without feeling threatened by it, since the characters on the screen act as a proxy for us.

All this is in service to the overarching message of the show, finally made explicit through a combination of all of these mimetic devices. At the end of Season 1.0, after all the interplay of Elliot's delusions of an imaginary friend and Mr. Robot, after the masks and deception of fsociety, the plan is enacted. Faced with the reality of this moment, Elliot is confronted by Mr. Robot. Elliot insists, to his imaginary friend, that Mr. Robot isn't real, to which Mr. Robot responds:

> Is any of it real? I mean, look at this! Look at it! A world built on fantasy. Synthetic emotions in the form of pills. Psychological warfare in the form of advertising. Mind-altering chemicals in the form of food. Brain-washing seminars in the form of media. Controlled isolated bubbles in the form of social networks. Real? ("eps1.9_zer0-day.avi")

Almost as though in direct argument against Plato, Mr. Robot insists that the distinction between reality and *mimesis* is far less clear than we would like to believe. Perhaps even worse, it's also not clear how much we care, considering the average consumer's penchant for self-indulgence and self-deception. In such a society, filled with such citizens, reality isn't quite what it's cracked up to be, and in such a world, a little *mimesis*, even in the form of an imaginary friend, might just be what we need to lead us to something even more real.

As Mr. Robot concludes: "You have to dig pretty deep, kiddo, before you can find anything real. We live in a kingdom of bullshit! A kingdom you've lived in for far too long. So, don't tell me about not being real! I'm no less real than the fucking beef patty in your Big Mac. As far as you're concerned, Elliot, I am very real. We are all together now, whether you like it or not" ("eps1.9_zer0-day.avi").

Indeed, we are all in this together, but whether or not we'll listen to our imaginary friends remains to be seen.

3
Click Bait for Black Fish

CHRISTOPHE POROT

Elliot and the philosopher Jean-Jacque Rousseau share one thing in common: according to both of them, "Man is born free and yet everywhere in chains."

However, despite the suspicious men in black suits, the way in which debt cripples life options, and Elliot's in-depth familiarity with the morally problematic behavior of many people, it's unclear how this subtle enslavement has come about.

What are the chains he is rebelling against, and how have they been wrapped on everyone's wrists? In trying to pin down the political theory that shapes the show, we can see that Elliot sees people, in part, as enslaved to themselves. Even further, some moments in the show suggest that the removal of this enslavement would be a contract that frees you from yourself.

If all of this is true, then *Mr. Robot* is a meditation on a concept that the intellectual historian Isaiah Berlin calls "Positive Liberty." Positive Liberty means that you can be enslaved to yourself and that you can be freed from yourself. This helps to explain the powerful presence of Elliot's most dangerous illusion, Mr. Robot, and helps us to make sense of the highly metaphorical dream sequence in which everyone, except for Elliot, is dining on a black fish.

Positive Liberty

Rousseau has the famous line that "man can be freed from himself." According to this view, someone can be enslaved to their lower, desirous form of themselves, and therefore must be freed from themselves from time to time.

For instance, we can imagine someone (let's call him Jim) wants to go on a diet; so Jim asks his friend, Bill, to help him out. He wants to go on a diet for reasons that he rationally sanctions: including the facts that eating poorly makes him irascible, unhealthy, and more easily fatigued. Thus, he asks Bill to help him stay on a diet and Bill consents to do so. Moments later, Jim sees a bowl of cookies and is overwhelmed by the ephemeral desire to eat one of them. As he reaches for the bowl, Bill pulls the bowl of cookies away from him and thereby frees Jim from himself. In this sense, he frees Jim from his lower desires and returns him to his rational self. Jim is unfree when he is acting on his lower desires and free when he is acting on his higher goals, according to this theory.

Positive Liberty is made possible by two basic ideas. First, it assumes that humans are divided between a higher, nobler (perhaps true) form of themselves and a lower, ignoble form of themselves. Second, it assumes that the lower (desire based) form of the self can operate as a slave master to the higher form of the self: therefore, when you're overwhelmed with desire you lack freedom. So, if freedom is understood as the ability to accomplish your goals, and your own weakness can prevent you from accomplishing those goals, then you can be enslaved from within. The only solution to this chained condition is to develop a contract where another person holds you to your higher self, and frees you from the lower self.

Elliot's Theory of Enslavement to Yourself

fsociety appears to be completely determined to free people from debt slavery. Their coded attack on E Corp undeniably attempts to loosen the hold that debt exercises over people's lives. In an fsociety video that Elliot did not participate in making, this notion of slavery is clearly spelled out: "We have delivered on our promise as expected. The people of the world who have been enslaved by you have been freed. Your financial data has been destroyed."

In this sense, to be free is to be free from debt, to be liberated from the way that financial obligations constrain our choices and constrain our world. But this does not perfectly explain the way Elliot looks at the world: even those in debt disgust him. He is, in many ways, repulsed by everyone around him and even repulsed by himself. If he simply felt bad for people because they were in debt, then the inflated, often condemning language, he uses about himself and others would simply make no sense.

Elliot uses his hacker skills to hunt people's lives, to see what they're up to and what they're really like. In one scene, he imagines everyone walking around the office with a sign attached to them that exposes their weaknesses and moral flaws: "I have had a nose job," "I cheat," "I steal." These are not the corporate overlords who have enslaved people through debt, this is the common citizen that Elliot is critiquing. I don't believe this reflects Elliot's sheer hatred of humanity. Instead, it contributes to his own crafting of an understanding of being enslaved to yourself.

Elliot sees people as partially enslaved to themselves. This notion is clarified when he discusses daemons: the invisible urges that control what we do. In "eps1.3_da3m0ns.mp4," Elliot elaborates on a particularly bizarre feature of humanity as he sees it:

> There's a saying. The devil's at his strongest while we're looking the other way, like a program running in the background silently, while we're busy doing other shit. Daemons, they call them. They perform action without user interaction. Monitoring, logging, notifications. Primal urges, repressed memories, unconscious habits. They're always there, always active. We can try to be right, we can try to be good. We can try to make a difference, but it's all bullshit. 'Cause intentions are irrelevant. They don't drive us. Daemons do. And me? I've got more than most.

Daemons are not imposed on us from the outside, they govern what we do from within. In the cookie example offered above, Jim's impulsive desire to take the cookie could be rephrased as a daemon taking control over his decision making skills. Intentions don't drive us—our higher goals and our higher self doesn't determine what we do. Instead it's the daemons who take control. Elliot even goes so far as to say that daemons seduce, manipulate, and own us. That sense of being owned by the daemon's echoes Rousseau's sentiment that "Obedience to appetite is mere slavery."

One of the most common examples of obedience to the lower self is addiction. To some, it represents being controlled from within: is the alcoholic truly free when they drink? Has the smoker chosen to smoke, or have they been forced to? According to Positive Liberty theorists, it is simply unfair to say that an addict is rationally choosing to continue squandering their health in obedience to their vice. It is therefore not a side note to the show that Elliot is an addict: it highlights his imprisonment from within. When he's trying to quit, Elliot emphatically declares his own unfreedom: "I can't control thoughts. I need this. I know I promised my last line, but ..." He needs his suboxone and morphine, he knows that the thoughts he has about those toxins is not under his rational control but, instead, is in control of his rationality.

Contract: Shayla and Mr. Robot

The description of daemons controlling people, of primal urges and base addictions governing life can seem bleak. It sounds like a recipe for hopelessness, a mere defense of traditional determinism. But this is not necessarily true: Rousseau's social contract was about reconciling the condition of man as chained to himself with the possibility of freedom. This freedom is achievable, at least partially, through contracts.

In the cookie example above, Jim had entered into a contract with his friend and his friend acted against Jim's lower self on behalf of his higher self. As political theorist Douglas

Casson explains it, if we vote to make drinking and driving illegal then we're voting to set up a force which will prevent our drunk selves from endangering the lives of others. We set up, in other words, a contract so that we might achieve our higher goals and behave in accordance with our true selves rather than our lower selves.

Elliot attempts to set up this kind of contractual relation to be freed from himself: he does so both in the real world and through his sheer imagination. The videos of Obama and Angela Merkel that hover in the background of the show clearly suggest that this series is set in modern America. However, modern America operates on a theory of freedom as personal choice—so long as you make the choice without someone physically stopping you, you are free. So Elliot cannot go through the state to achieve his individual freedom, instead he goes through his personal life and his imagination.

For his personal life, we could look to his relationship to Shayla (his drug dealer turned girlfriend from Season 1.0). Elliot's dealings with Shayla include a contractual element. He makes a contract with her to keep him on his structured regimen of morphine and suboxone. This is brought out when, after he desperately pleads for his drugs, she tells him "You made me promise never to give you these (morphine) unless I had your subs (suboxone)."

This conversation even veers into an explicit requirement to say "I promise" in order to finalize a new contract that will be enforced over Elliot regardless of his transitory desires. Elliot, vividly aware that daemons control his thoughts, set into motion a contract with Shayla that ensures she will not listen to him when they take over. But this is only a small feature of his relationship to Shayla, with whom he falls in love and whose death plunges him into a well of guilt.

His real source of freedom from himself comes in the dangerous illusion of Mr. Robot. Mr. Robot's role, as an instrument of freedom for Elliot, is identified in their first meeting. When Mr. Robot and Elliot are sitting in the subway Mr. Robot, who is a projection of Elliot's father, says "Your father was in prison, just like you are now . . . but I'm going to break you out." Therefore, Mr. Robot is immediately identified as an instrument of Elliot's freedom. But there is no visible prison that Elliot's locked into, no walls surrounding and limiting his movement, no one even coercing him into action (before Mr. Robot). Rather, the prison that Elliot endures comes from within: Mr. Robot notes that weakness was the problem his father has, and that Elliot now has.

In a scene that illuminates Mr. Robot's role as the enforcer of Elliot's contracts to himself, Mr. Robot pushes Elliot off a bridge. He does so because Elliot had failed to keep his word, "Your word is your bond" he says before punishing him in this terrifying moment. From then, it is clear that Mr. Robot is the agent of force who will act against Elliot when weaknesses and temptations prevent him from achieving the ends he commits to.

Mr. Robot's presence as a source of freedom is demonstrated time and time again throughout the series. First, the most obvious version of this, is Elliot's goal to free the world from debt-slavery. fsociety, their projects and goals, was set up by Elliot. But he feels that he is working for them partially out of interest and partially through obedience to Mr. Robot. Second, along the theme of addiction as slavery, it's Mr. Robot who carries Elliot through his recovery process.

When Elliot is trying to shake his addiction so that he can successfully hack E Corp's "Steel Mountain", he wakes up terrified by the prospect that he might be facing his Daemons on his own. Yelling, sweating, and shaking he cries out: "They all left. I'm alone! I'm alone!" Then Mr. Robot walks in and reassures him "No, you're not. I'm not going anywhere, kiddo. We're in this to the end." Elliot's slavery to addiction will not be overcome without Mr. Robot taking him to the end, ensuring he crosses the finish line. If freedom is understood as your ability to go from point A to point B and unfreedom understood as barriers that might stop you from doing this, then it's possible that some of those barriers are internal. The internal barriers, for Elliot, can only be overcome with external aid.

But why is Mr. Robot a projection of Elliot's father specifically? Surely there is an element of nostalgia and longing for what Elliot lost. However, it's also interesting to note that Positive Liberty has often been criticized as "paternal." The notion of the state involved in this theory of freedom has been critiqued, by Isaiah Berlin and others, as turning the state into a father figure who is disciplining his children. It seems to fit that Elliot's source of Positive Liberty is literally a father figure—disciplining and motivating him as though he is an unruly child.

Elliot's true father was nothing like Mr. Robot, as we saw in a flashback scene where Elliot is with his father at the video store. After Elliot steals money from a patron, his father doesn't punish him. His father takes him to a movie because he thinks Elliot is a good kid: the sense of force, the implementer of contracts and duty, is not symbolized by Elliot's real father. It is symbolized by the agent of his freedom, who works in ways and with a consistent dedication to contract that is paternalistic. Mr. Robot's existence is not merely about Elliot's father, it is about paternalism.

Elliot is living in a time and place that can hardly be described as paternalistic. But his deep commitment to the idea that he is enslaved from within may require him to imagine his way into freedom. Since the mechanisms to be "freed from yourself" are nowhere to be found in modern America, Elliot must do it on his own, as he says: "We all must deal with them (Daemons) alone." When Elliot laments having to face his daemons alone, it might be that he laments having to create, through sheer force of imagination, the external force that will free him from himself. Elliot, through Mr. Robot, does not only enforce contracts against himself, he does so with other members of fsociety. Recall when Romero starts to question the plan of fsociety, becomes afraid and tempted to back out. Mr. Robot, who was in fact Elliot, once again becomes the enforcer of contracts: With a gun to Romero's head, he yells: "You gave me your word when we started this thing that you'd finish it. I gave you my word what I'd do if you didn't."

Reverse Contracts, for Better or Worse

If it's possible to "force someone to be free" through a contract, then it seems equally possible to reverse this contract. In other words, to use someone's lower self against them. Elliot's aware of this possibility, and exploits it throughout the series. Elliot uses the analogy of hacking people to describe this process. In "1ps1.4_3xpl0its.wmv," he identifies different kinds of vices people are chained to, and he describes them as security flaws. The "glutton lacks discipline from his urges" and Elliot himself, as we have noted, says "I also have security flaws, I don't like being outside, I like morphine too much." Given these weaknesses, or security flaws, Elliot says "Hack the right person, people make the best malware. It's never hard to exploit most people." This is not a normal definition of exploitation; this is exploitation from within. Elliot believes that you can control people by enlarging the force and scope of their lower desires, by manipulating them through their own greed and hubris. Like hacking a computer, you can hack somebody from within their system.

Elliot's understanding of hacking people from within may sound like a mere Machiavellian scheme that he's capable of devising. But I believe it reconciles his otherwise disheartening commentary about people in the modern day with his critiques of capitalism, the internet, social media, and pills.

He believes that people have been hacked, and are continuing to be hacked. In an fsociety video, people are described as lost in a slumber and in need of being woken up: "If you have not yet woken up to the reality of profiteering from enslavement we've been warning you about, I hope you realize we are fast running out of time." What is this profiteering from enslavement? How can one profit from enslavement when those being enslaved are not enslaved in the common sense of the word? Mr. Robot elaborates on the content of that slumber in a stirring monologue at the end of Season 1.0. We live in:

a world built on fantasy. Synthetic emotions in the form of pills. Psychological warfare in the form of advertising. Mind-altering chemicals in the form of . . . food! Brainwashing seminars in the form of media. Controlled isolated bubbles in the form of social networks. Real? You want to talk about reality? We haven't lived in anything remotely close to it since the turn of the century. We turned it off, took out the batteries, snacked on a bag of GMOs while we tossed the remnants in the ever-expanding dumpster of the human condition. We live in branded houses trademarked by corporations built on bipolar numbers jumping up and down on digital displays, hypnotizing us into the biggest slumber mankind has ever seen.

So how does this make sense? How have people been hypnotized, how have they been tossed into this slumber from which they need to wake up? Why is the human condition a "dumpster"? If you look at the language of Mr. Robot's monologue it becomes clear. As far as I can tell, the point is that unchecked capitalism ultimately encourages companies to hack people, to tap into their addictions so that they keep buying products. This is how they profit from enslavement.

Let's start with food, which is described as the sale of "mind altering chemicals." It is fairly well established that sugars and fats are addictive: in fact, there is a multi-million member society called "Overeaters Anonymous." They use the same model of "alcoholics anonymous" to try to help people get over sugar addictions. When companies are selling soda, candy, and fast-food they are selling a product that can hack your brain. Sugar, like any other addiction, can override rational decision-making. The desire for profit might justify maximizing the level of an addictive substance in order to ensure people will keep buying more; so sodas and candies and lattes keep adding nearly absurd amounts of sugar into "food."

What about the media being described as "brainwashing" and advertising being described as "psychological warfare"? Advertising is a fascinating phenomenon: we live in an age full of free news, free entertainment, and free social media sites. However, they are free to users because we are the product being sold. The consumer is the advertiser. Human attention is the commodity that is sold to advertisers: this grounds the concept of "click bait." When websites receive a lot of visitors, which reveals how much attention they get, this determines how much they can charge for advertising. The more attention, the more advertising. So the very point of several sources of entertainment is precisely to get people to watch, or to visit a site. What is the easiest way to get people's attention? With entertainment that appeals to our daemons.

If news tries to be edifying rather than indulging your appetite for partisan commentary, then it probably won't get as many visitors. Syndicated columnist Nicolas Kristof noted in an interview with the *New York Times* that most extreme partisan sights are not owned by liberals or conservatives but rather owned by entrepreneurs seeking clicks so that they charge more for advertising. They've discovered that inflammatory titles matter more than truth content when clicks are the goal. So the industry developed around commodifying human attention could be recast as hacking people, as trying to get them addicted to a new form of entertainment so that they might sell human attention.

Thus, Elliot's damaging descriptions of modern people can be harmonized with his placing the blame for society's ills on corporate overlords. This condition is a product of having been hacked, of reversing the positive freedom contract, so that people can be controlled from within. Elliot understands the hacked existence to be the definition of "normal" in today's society. So, when he commits himself to being normal, he does so by indulging the hacks of sugar and social media: "I'll heart things on instagram. I'll drink vanilla lattes."

Black Fish

In the end, I believe Mr. Robot's role as an instrument of freedom and capitalism's role as a source of slavery is crystallized in a highly metaphorical dream sequence where everyone is eating "black fish." Elliot dreams of a conversation between him and a black fish, swimming around in a confined bowl. The fish describes his condition inside of the bowl as no different from prison; the fish becomes a symbol for being in prison.

After this conversation, the dream pivots to a scene where Elliot is back in his office, which has been turned into a restaurant. The black fish is being served, with pebbles from the bowl decorating the plate underneath it. Everyone is eating this fish but Elliot; we see a mother force feed the black fish to her child. We see his co-workers eat it. If you look at the location, the black fish dinner is placed where computers normally are (the center of the cubicles).

Elliot, however, does not eat the fish. He eats "Pop's Pie." Perhaps this means that everyone is being hacked by the black fish, who represents the reverse contract, but Elliot is trying to hack himself through the image of his father in Mr. Robot (Pop being the key term). Maybe Elliot is trying to be freed from himself through Mr. Robot, his Pop's pie, while he watches others dine on the blackfish. Elliot's friend and colleague Daisy tries to get him to join her, by saying "It's delicious" and offering him a piece of black fish. Elliot, of course, refuses because he does not want to be hacked.[1]

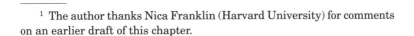

---

[1] The author thanks Nica Franklin (Harvard University) for comments on an earlier draft of this chapter.

II

Control Is an Illusion

4
The End of Privacy

Matthew William Brake

Hello Friend. I don't know if someone is actually reading this, or if I'm just making up an imaginary reader in my mind.

But if you are reading this, then you're like me. By sheer accident, you stumbled upon your new favorite TV show, *Mr. Robot*. In this show, viewers are introduced to the character of Elliot Alderson, a man with social anxiety issues who uses his hacking skills to violate the privacy of others in order to get to know them, sometimes leading him to take the law into his own hands and expose people who are involved in illegal activities.

Elliot's path leads him to encounter the hacktivist group, fsociety, who want to use Elliot's hacking skills to erase the record of all the debts held by the corporation E Corp (or "Evil" Corp). Elliot and fsociety attempt to create a new world by freeing people from the debts that financially enslave them to the corrupt managers of Evil Corp. While we may be sympathetic to Elliot and his cause, we also find his hacking of other people's private information morally problematic.

Privacy is a funny thing, isn't it? We can't imagine a just society without it, which is why we criticize NSA wiretaps, but while privacy protects our own personal information from those who might misuse it, it can also allow injustice to fester in the dark.

Thomas More, the Non-Sense Peddler, and Elliot

Don't worry, friend. I'll return to my point about privacy, but we have a long way to go before that.

In 1516, Sir Thomas More wrote a book entitled *Utopia* (actually, its official name is much, much longer). More wrote it as a fictitious thought experiment, exemplified by the very title of the book *Utopia*, meaning "No place." In the book, More recounts a conversation with a traveler he met named Raphael Hythloday, whose last name means something like "Non-sense Peddler." This nonsense peddler tells More about the laws and customs of the people on the island of "No Place."

Like Elliot, More himself seems to have been of two minds in this book. As you know, friend, Elliot suffers from delusions, and his psyche contains more than one personality: his own and that of his dead father, Mr. Robot. We're even tempted to add in ourselves as personalities inside Elliot's mind since we see events as they unfold from Elliot's unreliable perspective, all while he communicates with us, the viewers, and carries us with him through the events of the show. There is a fractured perspective within one mind.

Likewise, More and Hythloday seem to represent a split in More's own perspective, with Hythloday representing More's idealistic side and More's representation of himself in *Utopia* representing a pragmatic side that is willing to compromise.

While it's unlikely that More believed that Utopia represented the best commonwealth possible, it provided him with an opportunity to critique the social norms of his own day, including the injustice and greed in his own society, and to imagine a more just society. Hythloday is a part of More's personality that is unleashed and allowed to offer a scathing critique of English upper-class society that More's own character in the book refrains from doing. Hythloday makes it clear to More that he would never have left Utopia and come back to England if not for wanting to spread news of this island to others. In his own way, this could be his way of saying, "F&%$ society!"

A Conspiracy of the Rich and the Legality of Hacktivism

In the opening episode of *Mr. Robot*, Elliot tells us about a group of super-rich people, "the top one percent of the top one percent," who are "secretly running the world" (Hello, Friend). Elliot is referring to Evil Corp. They run the world and set the rules by which ordinary citizens have to live, and they hold a huge proportion of the population in what amounts to debt slavery.

The upper classes live in an abundance acquired on the backs of the labor and debt of others, like fsociety member Trenton's parents about whom he comments, "They're going to die in debt doing things they never wanted to do" ("eps1.6v1ew-s0urce.flv"). fsociety's plan is to take matters into its own hands by wiping Evil Corp's servers and freeing people from their debts.

We might question the illegal nature of hacktivism. We are a society governed by the "rule of law" after all. But what happens when those laws themselves do not further the cause of justice?

Hythloday takes this up in a discussion concerning the use of the death penalty for punishing theft in sixteenth-century England. Hythloday recounts a dinner at which a man noted his surprise at how thieves kept springing up despite the powerful deterrent of death by hanging. To this man, Hythloday notes the excessiveness of the punishment of death for theft while also making known the plight of the poor who have no work and no other way to survive. The man's response is equivalent to that of an older relative commenting about people on government welfare: "They could get a job if they wanted to."

Hythloday responds by pointing out the vulnerability of many workers, including those whose minds and bodies have been shattered by war, those who may be too old to learn a new trade, and those who are overlooked for someone who has been less weathered by life. Meanwhile, Hythloday points out, there are plenty of rich people who contribute nothing to society but simply live "off the labor of others," while raising the rent on these same laborers and bleeding them dry.

It is the laborers who cause society to function and without whom it "would simply cease to exist." However, Hythloday observes that working men (and women in our day) "sweat without reward or gain in the present but also agonise over the prospect of a penniless old age." At this point, we can think of Angela's father and the massive debt he found himself in at the end of his working years.

Not only does society take "the labor of their best years," but "when they are worn out by age" and sick, it forgets "all their sleepless nights and services" and cares little about whether they "die a miserable death."

To make matters worse, the rich attempt to "grind out of the poor part of their daily wages," not in secret meetings behind closed doors but "by public laws." The law, which should protect those who have the least, has been perverted to protect those who have the most. (Friend, pay attention now.) Hythloday then calls this "a conspiracy of the rich." Hythloday's words resonate with Elliot's comments about a secret group of super rich people controlling the world.

We see an actual conspiracy of the rich take place in *Mr. Robot*, one part of which specifically affects Elliot's life in a dramatic fashion. I am, of course, referring to the case of the 1993 Washington Township chemical leak. As you know, friend, this leak was responsible for the deaths of Elliot's father and Angela's mother, as well as twenty-four other employees of Evil Corp. The law was on the side of Evil Corp, which had indeed conspired to cover up their complicity in the incident. In a world where the rich hold the real power, even "the clearest matter in the world can be made cloudy and truth itself brought into question" through a legal loophole.

In this kind of world where the truth is buried so deeply and protected by the law, what can one do but break the law in order to bring the truth into the light of day? It was only by breaking the law that fsociety was able to make public the cover up of the Washington Township case, yet society is more likely to prosecute the hackers than the corporation that created the unjust conditions that led to the illegal hack. Likewise, Hythloday believes that the greed of a few ruins a society and creates the conditions whereby stealing to survive becomes necessary. England makes people thieves "and then punishes them for it." He also imagines a scenario in which famine kills many thousands of people and supposes that if afterward "the barns of the rich were searched," then one would find enough food to have saved the many poor who died so much that they never would have known that there was a food shortage.

Something is wrong with a world where blatant injustice can be covered up and the poor suffer and die while others around them live in luxury.

Money, Property, and Greed

Perhaps a conversation between Elliot and his psychiatrist Krista can shed some light on what is wrong with our world:

KRISTA: What is it about society that disappoints so much?

ELLIOT: [*in an internal monologue*] Oh, I don't know. Is it that we collectively thought Steve Jobs was a great man even when we knew he made billions off the backs of children? Or maybe it's that it feels like all our heroes are counterfeit. The world itself is just one big hoax. Spamming each other with our running commentary of bull#$%& masquerading as insight. Our social media faking intimacy. Or is it that we voted for this, not with our rigged elections, but *with our things, our property, our money*. I'm not saying anything new. We all know why we do this, not because *Hunger Games* books make us happy but because we want to be sedated. Because it's painful not to pretend. Because we're cowards. F@#$ society! ("eps1.0_hellofriend.mov," emphasis mine).

Elliot holds society responsible for its own ills, citing the power of private property and money for determining the type of society we live in.

Hythloday echoes Elliot's critique of his own society, believing that "wherever you have private property, and money is the measure of all things, it is hardly ever possible for a commonwealth to be just or prosperous." While people scramble to designate and protect their own private property, the endless numbers of lawsuits regarding property show how unnatural private ownership really is. Hythloday believes that a truly just society requires goods to be shared equally. Otherwise, no matter how plentiful goods are and how much people try to acquire as much as they can, "a handful of men end up sharing the whole pile, and the rest are left in poverty." To make matters worse, those who own this pile are "the worst citizens."

With this last description, it's hard not to think about Evil Corp and some of its executives: Phillip Price, Tyrell Wellick, and Terry Colby. Evil Corp owns seventy percent of credit worldwide, keeping many people in debt slavery. Price, Wellick, and Colby show themselves to be terrible human beings throughout the series. Price, the power hungry CEO of Evil Corp, implies that he was responsible for murdering his predecessor and also mocks the weakness of Evil Corp EVP of Technology James Plouffe when he commits suicide on live television. Tyrell Wellick, aside from the creepy BDSM relationship he has with his wife (also a major creep), is willing to do whatever it takes to increase his own power and influence, attempting to seduce and then murdering the wife of his competitor for the CTO position at Evil Corp. Finally, Terry Colby, when initially confronted by Angela about the cover-up of the Washington Township incident, invites her to perform a degrading sex act before meeting with her a second time and telling her, "At the end of the day, money will always be better than what you're looking for."

This is akin to the world that Hythloday sees in sixteenth-century England, and he doubts that any real justice is possible "as long as private property remains." To show that such a world is possible, he turns to the example of the Utopians, who have done away not only with private property, but privacy itself.

Privacy and Hacking Our Way to Utopia

See, friend, I told you I'd circle back to the issue of privacy. Were you worried? Were you concerned that I was leading you down a rabbit role that would take us far afield of where I started out? Don't be worried. It will all make sense now.

Hythloday appeals to the made-up island of Utopia to address the problem of private property and the accumulation of money. Regarding Utopia, he says, "There is nothing private anywhere."

In Utopia, even the entrances to people's houses are easily accessible, not keeping anybody out, and houses are exchanged every ten years. Everyone eats in common mess halls because enough is provided for everyone so that there is no reason for anyone to eat in private at home. In religious services, "everyone's public behavior is supervised." Before traveling, you must obtain permission, and people usually travel in groups. There are "no hiding places; no spots for secret meetings . . . they live in the full view of all."

A lack of such clandestine places can prevent those in power "from conspiring together to alter the government and enslave the people." A conspiracy of the rich can't take place when the rich are unable to hide behind the veil of privacy. This veil is what fsociety seeks to break through with their hacks.

You could argue that it is this veil of privacy that allows the very corruption we all disdain to grow and fester away from where any of us can see it, not just in corporate boardrooms and the halls of government power, but even in our own lives. The very right to privacy we think keeps us safe also allows multiple injustices in the world to be covered over.

In some ways, we're all like Elliot. We want the corruption in the world to be exposed, but we ourselves also feel alone and fragmented by the private worlds that separate us from each other. In Utopia, however, everyone is "at home everywhere." Hythloday says, "The whole island is like a single family." No one is doing meaningless work (like working at

Allsafe to protect Evil Corp's records) to protect the luxury and privacy of the rich and corrupt, but there are plenty of goods for everybody.

When fsociety finally succeeds in their plan to destroy all of Evil Corp's records, they do so while promising the inauguration of a new world, as Mr. Robot, wearing a mask, declares:

> Evil Corp, we have delivered on our promise as expected. The people of the world who have been enslaved by you have been freed. Your financial data has been destroyed. Any attempts to salvage it will be utterly futile. Face it: you have been owned. We at fsociety will smile as we watch you and your dark souls die. That means any money you owe these pigs has been forgiven by us, your friends at fsociety. The market's opening bell this morning will be the final death knell of Evil Corp. We hope as a new society rises from the ashes that you will forge a better world. A world that values the free people, a world where greed is not encouraged, a world that belongs to us again, a world changed forever. And while you do that, remember to repeat these words: "We are fsociety, we are finally free, we are finally awake!"

So maybe we should thank Elliot, Mr. Robot, and fsociety. And Anonymous. And Julian Assange. And Edward Snowden. Maybe they are helping to tear down the veil of privacy that allows injustice to be perpetuated in the world.

5/9 and Unintended Consequences

But wait, friend, before you start calling me a traitor. Or a communist. Not that I mind. You can think what you want. You're just a made-up reader in my mind anyway.

I want to remind you that Utopia is a work of fiction, and More has written it in a way that the moral superiority of Utopia isn't quite airtight. As I said earlier, More seems to divide his own opinion between two different characters, a version of himself and Hythloday. This divide represents More's practical and idealistic sides, but more importantly, it represents the reality that in any society there may be conflicting moral claims that require people to make difficult choices, the practical implementation of which may lead to unintended consequences.

After the 5/9 hack, the consequences of fsociety's actions weren't quite what they expected. The freedom they thought they would achieve quickly gave way to hardship for those they sought to help and a different form of social disruption than they intended. Meanwhile, the rich still conspired to further their own agenda, while the crumbling society negatively affected the very people fsociety sought to help.

So, friend, what can we say?

Perhaps only that any idealist dream should be cautiously implemented, for the practical effects of our good intentions may not produce the results that we intend.

It isn't that we shouldn't dream of a better world, and maybe the elimination of privacy would indeed lead to a more just world.

But here, More's voice is quite valuable, as he notes that some of the customs of Utopians are "really absurd" although there are "many features in our own societies that I would wish rather than expect to see."

In trying to create a more just society, we ought to be mindful of our inability to control the outcomes of our actions.

To my hacker friends who try to lift the veil of privacy in order to expose corruption, be careful that your Utopian dreams don't become a nightmare.

5
We Become the Grid

CHRISTOPHER KETCHAM

What do you know about Leviathan? Nothing? Good. You're not supposed to know. Does fsociety worry you? It worries me. Yet, they're just amateurs when put up against Leviathan. C'mon, stupid Guy Fawkes masks? Before we get to Leviathan there is the burning question we must all be asking.

Have we become the grid?

The military gave birth to packet switching technologies in the 1960s in the form of ARPANET. The idea was to continue the flow of information should the Russians kill various facilities with nuclear strikes. In other words, the military octopus could continue to communicate even if a few of its limbs were cut off. Duplicate data, split it up, send it on different journeys. Put it back together at the right node. Nothing is lost because it's replicated.

Well, the octopus has become a world-wide slime mold, gigantic, ubiquitous, duplicitous, interconnected, necessary, and for the most part free . . . sure. How do you define free?

What theoretical limit can anyone see for the grid as long as there are humans to feed it? It's sustenance of choice: information. Free information. The world has become honeycombed with server farms that produce and store like fat cells the edible nourishment for the internet . . . information. If the grid is everywhere, how much control does it have?

All your appliances. Like Darlene's house that goes haywire at the beginning of Season 2.0.

Information

Soon there will be nothing important that is not connected to or feeding, feeding the Leviathan.

—Anonymous

Thomas Hobbes saw war as the state of nature, everyone out for themselves. The grid was born in cold war where mutual assured destruction kept both Russia and the US from slitting each other's throats in a zero-sum game. Then, with the internet everything devolved further into anarchy, even deeper into the state of nature. No one has control; everyone can be out for themselves. However, that is changing.

Hobbes's Leviathan is the absolute ruler, the one for whom you have awe which is why you obey Leviathan and conform to the state of laws. The 1% x 1%, those who will control the hackverse, will become the Leviathan. fsociety is the feeble first step on the path to Leviathan.

You today hold the power of the grid in awe—thinking that it is yours, but it's not. It won't be free, because the absolute ruler, Leviathan will become your ruler. You see, fsociety will learn as it has with Elliot, that the blunt tactics of releasing debt by blowing up data storage facilities won't fly. They think they control Elliot, but do they?

So, will Leviathan be more like the five families of the New York mob? You think Russians and Ukrainians won't want to backdoor each other? Chaos! Brings nothing but heat. Dark Army? No. No. No. The Leviathan will be smarter than all of these. They aren't hackers for hire, vendetta coders; they have no desire for petty squabbles over who controls the sex sites. These tactics will not be their modus operendi. Zombie master of the botnet? No, it isn't denial of service . . . it's the control of the service.

Control of you, of your world. Yes. The world. How? Easier than you might think. Says Tyrell in the second season opener as Elliot's code is propagating though Evil Corp, "It's almost as if something's come alive."

Control

"How do we know we are in control?" Elliot asks his shrink in the second episode of Season 1.0.

Think about your own existence. There's information in your head. How did it get there? From information in the world. What if you were born in a locked in state, no senses at all. What would you become? Frightening thought. Thank the world for nurturing parents, school and, of course, the grid. Martin Heidegger called this the ready to hand world of your experience. Ready and in your hand for you to use. The grid you holster, pocket, carry and consult through any number of portals or devices each day. It has become as much a part of you as you . . . Ready to hand, right? But have we become the grid?

> Leon, hey Leon, it isn't *Seinfeld* anymore. Can't you see that? Well you can Leon, you can see it. I can see it in your eyes. They already have you.

In one recent study people were falsely told that there was a video of the 9/11 Flight 93 crash in Pennsylvania. When asked later if they remembered that video, many said they did. Even more problematic, there was a higher incidence of false memory if the person was age twelve or less on 9/11. The upshot is that if we can create false memories for you today, Leviathan might ultimately create your childhood for you and run it as a series. Your own *Word Up Wednesdays*. That is, until the series is canceled.

We Are the Grid and It Is Us

Mr. Robot explores the sinister side of the grid . . . As if false memories aren't sinister! Today, hackverse is a place to do some vandalism, to tag the walls of society, to wreck someone else's grid experience or even their lives. Sometimes this is to extort money and sometimes to release sensitive information for one cause or another. Elliot hates; but he is also a dreamer, an enforcer of what he sees wrong in the world—a rogue operative. He's not new. No, he's recycled code.

A decade before the world wide web, in 1982, William Gibson in his short story *Burning Chrome* had Automatic Jack and Bobby Quine burn Chrome, the money launderer for the mob. Hackers, dreamers, Bobby in love with a woman who happens to work for Chrome and wants money to impress her. Sure they burn Chrome, but does Bobby get the girl? Nope. Sloppy, sloppy. Single goal, money, retribution, name recognition, the thrill of the hack. Not our Leviathan. You won't see Leviathan burn Chrome. In this same story Gibson invents the word cyberspace, the illusion, the hallucination of being in the grid. How close are we? Close, a 5/9 hack close.

Replacing the external bombs that would have flattened hard-wired cities in the Cold War, hackverse infects the grid with influenza that flames certain nodes and shut down others. Information continues to flow despite these worms, Trojans, and virus attacks. New immune defenses are fashioned and the cold code of hackverse evolves as do the real viruses in the world.

Leviathan is more like a genetic disease. You're going along great until your genes kick in. Then you begin to fade. But see, you won't know you have the errant gene because it will simply appear, grafted onto the grid without so much as a sigh or a ripple in the fabric of space-time, cyberspace time, that is, the illusion of being inside. We hear Elliot, whose delusion illusion in the midst of Season 2.0 is now about complete, at the end of "eps2.5_h4ndshake.sme" implore us, "I'd like it if we could trust each other again." Fat chance of that happening, pal.

Grid Anatomy and Physiology

The grid is all that we are. Like us, it consumes, thinks, farts, defecates, and screws. It runs; it walks. It doesn't die when

Facebook members die. It just cryogenically freezes the detritus from the member and lets mourners offer their peace.

After a while the account of the deceased becomes like the tomb of our ancestor, words, decay, and perhaps a nice selfie scene or two. Maybe it's taken down from public view as would the tombstone that falls over or becomes so covered with lichen and mold it cannot be read. Yet it's still there.

The grid are us and we are the grid.

Today's hackers are lame. You know it. They try to steal your goods, everything that makes you who you are: your passwords, your social security number, your browsing history, your last physical, all which they can extort for blackmail or just make you look really bogus if you have a public persona. They want your money in other ways through credit card numbers, and passwords to your bank accounts. Government and institutional hackers have done some pretty amazing things like make nuclear centrifuges spin so fast they destroy themselves. This is only the tip of the iceberg.

A Hackish Moment

What if the grid could change you, rewire your external brain in the world so that your brain in your head is permanently changed? What amount of bogosity would it take for you to change your mind on anything from the upcoming election, to where you now prefer crufty clothing, or to frobnicate your favorite beverage so that you can't stand it anymore, or to make you watch frog television shows. Not quite as lame as blackmail or stealing, but we haven't made the best use of the hack.

You don't speak Hackish? Good. They're going to FTP you from your virgin grid moment until they wheel your final crash. They will grind grok friends for you, gun your significant other for someone they prefer for you: a loser. Hackverse will take over your world and make you work for it . . . for them? You become their best jock programmer. You have become a user, pal. They own you; they wheel you! And you don't even know it.

When you log onto that dating website you won't have to fill out any annoying questionnaires. Leviathan already knows who it wants you to date. You are presented with the array of lovelies or handsomes that meet their expectations for who you will become. Perhaps Leviathan needs blue-eyed blonde babies. Well, there you go. Or perhaps you who think you are going to be a CEO are going to get the alcoholic spouse who makes a fool of you at company functions. You see, Leviathan has already decided you won't become CEO. They won't let you. They have someone else for that. You languish in a back office shuffling paper.

Pshaw, Ain't Happening, Friend

Of course it could happen today. All Leviathan needs is to get your health records, have the dentist swab for DNA, and have all of your connected world in their database to algorithm into what it is they want you to become. It only takes a hack or two.

Leviathan never guesses, it knows. It plans, it schemes, and it controls your world. Don't you just hate it when you go to a web page after having looked at blenders and find ads for different makes and models of blenders every time you open a new web page? You looked up something on Amazon. Now they have it on your favorites reading list and so, here, read these others. Ah, Leviathan, you say. Not yet, but soon. You won't even blink an eye when you buy that blender and order the whole genre from Amazon. Did you really check the box to let Google provide you an "enhanced ad experience"? You did, didn't you?

You won't know Leviathan because, as Mr. Robot says, they won't slip up because, "Our encryption is the real world." He's on the right track, but Leviathan is more secure and invisible. They know how others get caught and won't do the same things. So, why not just wipe everyone's debt to Evil Corp? Spoiler alert!

Leviathan would not have permitted Evil Corp to become so powerful unless it wanted it to be powerful. For what purpose would Leviathan want Evil Corp to be powerful? Control. You who have massive school debt, you can't buy that car of your dreams. You weren't supposed to. They cost your parents their jobs when you were in high school so they had to burn through all the money that they had saved for your college. Leviathan even then didn't want you to buy the car of your dreams.

Your spouse, well, that too was part of the equation. That job you have? That too. They needed more of what you do, and this, of course, is also keeping you from getting that dream car. Surprise, all your kids are blue eyed and blonde as is your spouse. Coincidence? Leviathan. Tell me now, are you the grid or is the grid you?

I Think, Therefore . . .

What did René Descartes say? How could he know whether anything was real? What if an evil demon was making things happen?

How do you know? Are you like Neo from *The Matrix* who feels the difference between reality and his own machine existence? No, you are the subaltern now, the slave—just as Neo was, but not to machines that have run amok, but to your fellow humans of the hackverse, Leviathan.

How do detectives work? They gather evidence, put it on a wall and stare at it. They get their analog brain to working and months, maybe even years later the answer pops into their head. This is gonna happen a lot faster than that.

Look at what Elliot, a detective in his own way, did to Ron with a few bits of information in Ron's coffee shop in the first episode. What kind of algorithms do you think Leviathan is going to have? Killer ones.

With Ron, Elliot didn't have to work that hard except to hack Ron's porn site. He just gleaned all the traffic at the shop's Wi-Fi and sifted. Voilà!—child porn. Takedown! Elliot, however, is a loose cannon. He doesn't want money. He's socially challenged (fucking twisted) and he crashes through the grid like Ebola, violently destroying, leaving a bloody mess behind. He fears the 1% x 1% who own the hackverse already. He should. Leviathan is coming.

The 1% x 1% see rogues as what they are: Ebola. They deserve to be quarantined and then expunged from the Earth. Don't think of the future as being like a gross hack today where someone gets pissed off at a major corporation and takes their servers down with a denial of service attack. That's like bashing someone's head in with a sledgehammer in front of the sheriff. No, it is as Elliot says, it's going to be the 1% x 1% who hold the grid in their hands. You won't even notice when Leviathan ascends. Leviathan will be self-encrypted, polymorphic and you will be keylogged your whole life—in case you get any ideas of your own.

Cola Wars Revisited

It's gonna be subtle at first.

Fizzy Cola wants to beat Fuzzy Cola. So they pay the 1% x 1% to do things, subtle things. Hackverse puts out false taste tests and polls that give Fizzy the edge over Fuzzy. It is so under the radar that Fuzzy has no clue this is happening. Then there are stories of how bad Fuzzy is for you because it has preservatives that are linked to cancer in lab rats and makes kids obese. Fuzzy delivery drivers run out of gas because their satellite-connected electronic fuel gauges are tampered with and cases explode because their air conditioners malfunction and the stuff freezes . . . Just a little bit at a time . . .

After a while Fizzy has twice as much shelf space as Fuzzy. Fuzzy still is thinking they have to advertise more, but the ad counters are hacked. Fuzzy pays for thousands of ads that never make it to the pages. Fuzzy hits are higher than ever, but these are all so much vaporware. All in good time. All in good time. Elliot sees two pictures in his shrink's waiting room, "Coke or Pepsi?" What do you think?

Leviathan won't need to do any of this. Fizzy was always number one. Period. If you drink Fizzy, it is because you are meant to. Elliot, thinks he sees things. He's supposed to.

That's how they control someone as smart and as savvy as he is, by keeping him guessing all the time. He's being followed. That's all part of the plan to keep him in a state where he thinks he's losing it. His shrink? She was chosen because she can only go so far. She doesn't have the skills to talk away those pesky hallucinations.

Three Seconds to Jacking, Jack

Leviathan will give billions to neurobiological departments at the best universities to develop jack devices to plug their own warped brains into the grid. They won't tell the universities this. It isn't from Leviathan, you see, but from mega donors who have been convinced through neurologically challenged kids of their own that science can repair their broken brains. How did they get so broken? Leviathan understands genetics. Once the jack is made to help kids with profound brain damage, Leviathan quietly takes it to jack their minions in to the grid.

Jacking in is not a substitute for the supercomputers they buy with Fizzy money—supers are so much faster in crunching numbers. No these jackers are detectives, thinkers, seers, looking not for weaknesses in firewalls but for where people can be exploited. Leviathan has the tools, the code, and the AI to do most things, but it still needs humans to understand humans. The jackers are born not made. They're grown so that they don't burn up in the grid. Their minds can survive the super-speed and instant acceleration to ten gigaflops. They bounce off walls, dead ends, and speed through thick strands of cyberspace like the Silver Surfer does through the universe. They've learned how to target, focus, seek, and pause. They're waiting, listening to the grid for opportunities. Ah, jacker 147J60nP has found something.

Diamonds in a mid-continent African republic. In that country is a democratic leader who is beloved. Well, wouldn't you know it after a regular audit, irregularities: bribes, graft, corruption. Beloved democratic leader is flamed. On the scene comes Leviathan's cyberpunk. Well he is just the thing to solve that corruption problem. He's done it before. Perhaps he has, or maybe the stories are all hacked. How do you know, Mr. Descartes? Cyberpunk is elected and declares martial law. He nationalizes the diamond trade and sells diamonds at discount to Leviathan. Everyone—I mean Cyberpunk and Leviathan are happy. The people in diamond country are happy for a time to see corruption dealt with so swiftly. It starts slowly, the decline in quality of life. Curfews, police raids, disappearance of dissidents, meagre store shelves. It starts slowly—and it was surely meant to be.

How soon are we to the jackers, those who can plug their minds into the grid directly? We have people jacked into devices to help them hear and see. We have crude ones helping their hearts beat at a regular rate. It's all about electricity, now isn't it? Elliot has left the world, or perhaps never was in it to begin with. He knows he could live in the grid; he vicariously does today. He won't be someone they let jack in. Why? He doesn't care about power or money, only destruction and his own warped sense of justice. He will never get the opportunity to jack in . . . that is unless he can hack the jack. What's the deal with Elliot's lucid dreaming near the end of season two? You think he already has hacked a jack?

The 1% x 1% fear Ebolas like Elliot because the invisibility of their own Janus face can be writ live by someone like Elliot. Leviathan would not let Elliot grow to maturity. End of show.

Jacking is not the singularity, the artificial intelligence convergence that Ray Kurzweil and others say is coming. It goes beyond. It begins like Neo, connected electronically to the grid through a headset or a permanent plug. It will evolve as Leviathan tasks the labs and universities to find permanence for life in the grid. It is the symbiont of DNA and electronic data that begs to be discovered and then deployed. It is the merger of the Mechanist ideal of the machine with the Shapers' ideal of the gene, from warring factions in the universe that Bruce Sterling warned us about in his *Crystal Express*.

It isn't the rise of the machine at the expense of the human. Rather it's a merger of equals to better both . . . Elliot's companion, the one he talks to? I wonder. Robin Hanson in *The Age of Em* envisions whole brain emulations populating the grid in the not too distant future. Think copying your mind and putting it into the machine electronically, then setting it loose. Change your passwords now! Too late. Your doppelganger has already taken over all your accounts.

Leviathan Breathes

How does Leviathan benefit from all this? Power, control, money. They'll build industries they need and erase others that they alone find lame. They'll take revenge out on a particular class or race of people or a particular culture or even city. Why? They have their reasons.

"Let's make Detroit a bitchin place." They keep others away from the nicest places to visit by disinformation so that that the 1% x 1% of Leviathan can enjoy the view. Bring forward Miami reports and pictures of chronic toxic algae blooms, permanent zika outbreaks, and open gang warfare in the streets. Rather than go to warm sunny Miami, you believe it is better to be in cold gloomy and deteriorating Detroit. You see, hackers don't need to make Detroit any better, just make you think that way. They, of course, have taken over the mansions of Miami and live like Al Capone—you know nothing of this.

Remember the *Maine*

Hell, you know this can happen. How do you think we got into the war with Spain over Cuba? In 1898, the USS Battleship *Maine* blew up in Havana harbor and William Randolph Hearst, yes the publisher, had a field day in his papers making the thing look like the Spanish did it. Did they? Who knows? Anyway, when the war was in full blossom Teddy Roosevelt made his famous charge up San Juan Hill, and later became Vice President and when McKinley was killed became President. Coincidence?

Hearst was a hacker in the analog world before computers. Can you imagine what today's hackers could have done? Who knows what would have happened? Roosevelt, you remember wasn't really McKinley's first choice, but he was making waves to break up the trusts as governor of New York. So the trusts figured the best way to make Roosevelt go away was to make him Vice President. Think of how smoothly the hackverse could make such a thing happen today. Why break up the trusts? Well, Rockefeller made more money from stock in his shorn subsidiaries than he ever did when he had the whole barrel of oil to himself. What difference is there between the 1% x 1% of the 1890s: Carnegie, Vanderbilt, Rockefeller, and Melon, and the 1% x 1% of Leviathan? Not much, other than the Janus cloak of invisibility of Leviathan's 1% x 1%.

They put up their own candidates to legitimize what they do and set up whole countries where legislation is conducted outside of public view. They have you arrested on trumped up charges just because you say something they don't like. They are the shadow government you will not even know exists because all dissent disappears like so much of yesterday's garbage. Mr. Robot never guesses, he knows.

Leviathan creates a cybercosmos where they are the black hole. Everything revolves around them. There is nothing that can escape them should they want to devour it. Even in a black hole information doesn't disappear; according to Hawking it bubbles out when the black hole evaporates. But like a black hole Leviathan lets no light of day shine upon it. Leviathan is made invisible by their cloak of Gyges, not a gravity cloak but a cloak of invisibility. You see, it isn't about bugs anymore. There are no bugs except for bugs Leviathan has introduced. Leviathan has become the Grid. It is self-repairing, self-replicating, ubiquitous, omnivorous, omnipresent, and omniscient.

"Behold, I am the light of the world."

6
Who Has the Power?

HEIDI SAMUELSON

In a revealing conversation at the beginning of the tenth episode of Season Two, Phillip Price, CEO of E Corp, known derogatorily as "Evil Corp," reveals that his sole motivation in life is always to be the most powerful person in the room:

> In my life, as I was making my way, I always asked the question, am I the most powerful person in the room? The answer needed to be yes. To this day, I still ask that question. And the answer is still yes. In every room in the entire world, the answer is 'yes', with the exception of one. Or two. And that drives me.

As CEO of E Corp, which manufactures personal computing technology and owns seventy percent of the global consumer credit industry, he does seem to be one of the most powerful people in the world. Even after the 5/9 hack, which was meant to destabilize financial markets and redistribute wealth, Price seems convinced that E Corp and its new currency will prevail, and he remains at the company's helm. But what does he mean by power? Does he really have it? And who are these one or two people in the world he thinks are competing with him?

Philosopher Michel Foucault (1926–1984) wrote extensively on power and different types of power. And one of the most crucial features of power for Foucault, which throws a wrench in Price's plan, is that power is not something that can be possessed by a person. Power is something that operates. What that means is that power works through social institutions and social practices. Power is in how we relate to things, how we talk about things, and how truth is created through our actions and words. Power isn't something we control.

According to Foucault, power has worked differently over the course of history. People used to have to answer to kings or central authority figures, and these kings had the power over the life and death of their subjects. Foucault refers to that type of power as "sovereign power." This might be the type of power that Price is talking about, the type of power that would generate awe and fear in a room, but, according to Foucault, in the eighteenth and nineteenth centuries, a different power emerged—disciplinary power.

With disciplinary power, people—right down to our bodies—are regulated by rules and social norms that work without any one person in charge of them. We even regulate ourselves. We live in "disciplinary societies," where the way things are organized reflects this social form of power. Say you work for Allsafe Cybersecurity. The way the cubicles are arranged in your office—so anyone can see what you are working on if they walk by—is due to disciplinary power. When you're sitting at your computer, you feel like you're constantly being watched, and the accompanying fear of exposure forces you to stay on task. It's disciplinary power at work.

To convince Price that this is how power works in contemporary society, it would be helpful to look at some of the other ways that Foucault says disciplinary power appears. Let's look at some of the other people Price might think are competing with him for power.

Elliot and the Panopticon

First, look at Elliot Alderson. In the opening sequence of Season One of *Mr. Robot*, Elliot says to the viewer:

> There's a powerful group of people out there that are secretly run-
> ning the world. I'm talking about the guys no one knows about, the
> guys that are invisible, the top one percent of the top one percent,
> the guys that play god without permission.

He believes these men are watching him, and he thinks they
got wise to him after he hacked and then confronted a pedophile
who was running a massive child pornography web service.

Here, Elliot also equates power with control. But if these
people do "play god without permission," they sound more
like an example of Foucault's sovereign power. Foucault uses
the example of a king, but the only necessary feature of the
sovereign is that they are a central authority figure with the
power of life and death over people. Though the men suppos-
edly after Elliot might be trying to kill him, which would be
them using the power over life and death, the men in suits
are anonymous, not centralized. These men seem more like
they operate with disciplinary power, which is a decentralized form of power.

One of the key features of disciplinary power is surveillance. Foucault uses an example from another philosopher,
Jeremy Bentham (1747–1832), to explain how this surveillance works. Bentham wrote about a building structure
called a "panopticon" that he thought could be used for prisons and other institutions. In the panoptic prison, the prison
cells form a ring making up the outside of the building, and
there is a watchtower in the middle where officers and in-
spectors are concealed from view but can see out in all direc-
tions. Because prisoners think they are being watched, they
will follow the rules and won't cause problems because they
fear punishment. Though Bentham was referring to prisons,
Foucault used the principle behind it—anonymous surveillance (or the illusion of surveillance) and normalization
(changing behavior due to the surveillance)—to apply to disciplinary societies, including in spaces like the cube farm at
Allsafe Cybersecurity, where Elliot works.

In spite of his paranoia and unreliability as a narrator,
we know that Elliot *is* likely being watched, and we see this

confirmed in Season Two. He and other members of fsociety have been watched at the very least by the FBI, if not by others. But, for Foucault, surveillance doesn't make particular people powerful—even the FBI. The point of the panopticon is that we *feel* like we're being watched all the time, by anyone and everyone, and this is enough to affect how we act. We see this at Allsafe when people can come up to Elliot and interrupt him from his work. We see this feed into Elliot's own mental instability.

You don't need to be in the FBI or be a member of the ultra-elite to watch people. Elliot himself, though a victim of surveillance, is a hacker. He hacks everyone from pedophiles to a man his therapist dates. Through ISPs, through stored data, through numerous electronic surveillance techniques, Elliot can not only watch other people, but he can use that information to understand and predict their behavior. Surveillance can turn on those who surveil—Elliot's sister Darlene Alderson, a hacker in her own right and a member of fsociety, uses surveillance in Season 2.0 when she orchestrates a hack into the FBI.

It's more complicated than this, because Elliot isn't just any hacker. In fact, Elliot isn't just Elliot. He's also Mr. Robot. By orchestrating the 5/9 hack and then the mysterious "Phase Two," Elliot, acting as Mr. Robot, has demonstrated what seems like the sort of power he mentioned from the outset. He could very well be the "one" Price is talking about. But does he really have power? Do the one percent of the one percent?

In a disciplinary system, no one has power. They might think they have power, but the power of surveillance isn't held in any one person's hands, and we can see this because it's available to everyone from the FBI to an Adderall addict with massive identity issues. Hacker groups recognize this dispersed power of surveillance when they maintain anonymity. They don't hide their identities because hacking is illegal; they do it because the internet is the modern-day panopticon.

Angela and Biopower

Angela Moss also catches the eye of Price, so let's consider her potential power next. Angela's mother and Elliot and Darlene's father died from leukemia caused by a toxic waste leak from an E Corp chemical plant in Washington Township, NJ. The leak was willfully orchestrated and then covered up by E Corp, even though they were aware of the health risks. In the first two seasons of *Mr. Robot*, Angela attempts to use everything from litigation to blackmail to getting a job at E Corp all to try to force E Corp to admit to wrong-doing.

What Angela is attempting to fight against is the pervasive type of power in a disciplinary society that Foucault calls "biopower." Foucault explains in *The History of Sexuality* that biopower refers to the practices of modern social and political institutions to exercise power over life, or "the living bodies of persons." Biopower works through forms of social control over our bodies that we might not even be aware of. This clearly happens in the physical discipline required for military training, but it also happens in schools and workplaces where we must sit still in one place for hours on end and right down to the way that public bathrooms are organized by gender. Biopower can be seen in the booming business of pharmaceuticals, with the stigma of suicide, and with healthcare being considered an industry instead of a service.

E Corp decided to cover up their involvement in polluting a water system at the expense of lives, which seems like the sovereign power of life over death. But E Corp covered it up. They didn't admit to it or take responsibility for it, which is actually more like the anonymous workings of biopower. They failed to keep Angela's mother (and Elliot and Darlene's father) alive. Even though biopower typically aims to keep people alive, E Corp did demonstrate social control over the bodies of the people they poisoned with the leak. When Angela confronts Terry Colby, the CTO of E Corp, about the leak, she uses information about the pending litigation on him as a bargaining chip to get him to admit to wrongdoing.

And he does admit to her that a few people in a board room—while eating shrimp cocktail—decided to hide evidence and documents that implicated them in the leak, because it was worth the benefit to them and their corporation.

These men are not punished for the leak or cover-up, in spite of Angela's attempt to make a deal. Arguably, one of the reasons they aren't punished is because they were operating within what is to be expected out of biopower. The power over life and death is decentralized, and untimely death goes against the aim to keep people alive, so it makes sense that no one would be held accountable. Death in this case would be seen as an accident to anyone in a regime of biopower, and so they hardly even need to do any covering up.

Though Angela herself never toys with life and death, she attempts to counter the biopower that failed to keep her mother alive by seeking to find someone to take blame. When that doesn't go as planned, in Season Two, she gets a job with E Corp. Seeming to not hold a grudge against the company, or perhaps using it to her advantage, she eventually asks to be put in the Risk Management division so she can get access to the Washington Township case files. Though Angela's motives are never fully clear, she attempts to make someone be held responsible for what seems like an act of sovereign power committed in a system run on biopower.

Angela gives up the fight, though, when she's kidnapped by the Dark Army and given a series of psychological screening questions until Whiterose finds her worthy to talk to. Whiterose convinces Angela not to reveal incriminating files in the Washington Township case and also that she knew about Angela's mom and Elliot and Darlene's dad's death. Whiterose insists that they died "to take humanity to the next level." Whatever Angela hears in this message is enough for her to cut ties with her lawyer. Once again, we find her confronting biopower, because whatever taking humanity to the next level means, life is not in the hands of a sovereign.

Do her attempts to fight the system of biopower make Angela powerful? Angela does seem interested in the type of power that Price appears to have. But ultimately she's trying to fit a modern world that operates with biopower into a model of sovereign power, and it won't work. Foucault does claim that some mechanisms of sovereign power continue to remain in our time, but in limited ways and always entangled with biopower.

Whiterose and Power-Knowledge

Out of all the characters in Mr. Robot, Whiterose seems to be the most likely candidate for the one person more powerful than Price. In fact, Whiterose appears to have power in two ways—as the leader of the Dark Army, a hacker collective based in China, and as Minister Zheng, the Chinese Minister of State Security. In a meeting between Zheng and Price, Price seems unclear about what Zheng is planning, and he doesn't think Zheng is doing enough to help, which indicates that he thinks Zheng has power to wield. But does Whiterose possess the type of power that Price thinks?

In Season 1.0, Whiterose is a mysterious figure, much like the Dark Army she appears to lead. Little is revealed about the Dark Army to the viewer, but we learn that they are dangerous and unforgiving, because the members of fsociety are afraid of them and hesitant to work with them. In Season One, episode 8, when it seems like the 5/9 hack is still on, Whiterose meets with Elliot, but only for three minutes. In that three-minute conversation, she gets Elliot to agree to disable the honeypot that Gideon installed in Allsafe's network as a precaution after the E Corp hack—a piece of knowledge that Elliot didn't have.

Whiterose herself operates with what Foucault calls "power-knowledge." Power and knowledge are related, but both are relative, unstable, and systemic. Power itself doesn't have any intention or aim; it operates in the world using knowledge that we think is true. Mechanisms of power can produce knowledge that makes use of information about people and what they do. It can create the way we talk about something to the point where certain ideas get internalized and affect our behavior in the world. This means that people will correct themselves to adhere to particular norms, which means that they use knowledge to govern themselves independently of any one person or central power telling them what to do.

It seems like Whiterose wields power by having access to government information, and she clearly has some end in mind, although it's unknown to us as viewers. But, Foucault claims that knowledge is reproduced and shaped in accordance with anonymous intentions. Like a game of telephone, the spread of knowledge cannot really be controlled. So, although it seems like Whiterose must possess a great deal of knowledge, power-knowledge still operates anonymously. It doesn't really matter who has the knowledge. Once again, the Dark Army proves this. We don't know the identity of anyone in the Dark Army other than Whiterose. Allegedly they have ties to Iran, Russia, and North Korea, but their individual identities are anonymous, and their organization is compartmentalized. It's unlikely that Whiterose knows who they are either.

Even though Whiterose seems to be in the center of the 5/9 hack, Phase Two, and Price's plans for E Corp, whatever knowledge she has isn't the same as power. And sometimes trying to wield knowledge is useless. We find out at the end of Season Two that the FBI, particularly Agent "Dom" DiPierro, knows quite a bit more about Elliot and fsociety than Dom let on. Though she possesses a bulletin board with arrows, has Darlene in custody, and knows that everything points to Elliot, Dom doesn't seem to have power either. Even with the knowledge, she seems out of control, marginalized, and not listened to by her peers, which shows that factors other than just having knowledge are at play.

Likewise, the knowledge Whiterose seems to have is dispersed. As much as she seems to orchestrate things, as Whiterose and as Zheng, we mostly see her as a conduit for plans that operate with a lot of people, with different local agendas and local knowledge independent of hers, spread out all over the world. Even though Price seems to respect Zheng as an equal, Zheng-Whiterose isn't a sovereign, and so ultimately she's replaceable.

Does Phillip Price Have Power?

Phillip Price seems like he wields power as the CEO of E Corp. And in a capitalistic society, we tend to associate wealth with power. But in the aftermath of the 5/9 hack, not only does he not seem concerned with the fate of E Corp, he is seen in the last scene of Season One having a conversation with Zheng sitting comfortably in front of a roaring fire. It is unclear whether Price knew about the hack beforehand or profited from it, due to the mystery surrounding both his and Zheng-Whiterose's character, but he clearly was not suffering from it.

In Season 2.0, we see that part of his plan for power involves introducing ECoin—a virtual currency to replace traditional currency, harmed by the 5/9 hack. By introducing a new currency, he can restart the process that made him rich with traditional currency, but now with ECoin. But does this do anything other than make him rich?

E Corp is, among other things, a tech company. Technology is one way the idea of the panopticon operates in our everyday lives. Through data collection on social media that produces targeted advertising, to tech giants having access to your computer's camera or your cell phone's microphone, to CCTV in major cities, the constant surveillance of the panopticon is closer to a reality than Foucault knew at the time of his death in 1984. Because technology enables much of this surveillance, it seems that the people at the helms of tech companies, like Price, are the ones with the power, but the point of all these forms of disciplinary power is that power is dispersed. Phillip Price is not the one watching you—anyone could be watching you. Anyone can be a hacker.

What Phillip Price thinks of as power and what we think of as knowledge are actually social structures, sources of social control, and, ultimately, these institutions deinstitutionalize power. Contemporary forms of disciplinary organization allow large numbers of people to be controlled by ever smaller numbers of "experts," like Zheng or Price, but they are mere conduits of power. Power is exercised through disciplinary means via various social institutions like schools and office buildings and in the dependency on certain financial institutions like ECoin. Power is in the prison, in the cube farm at Allsafe, in the security fortress at Steel Mountain.

What Phillip Price fails to recognize is that the people at the head of these institutions that operate with disciplinary power don't really matter. Power operates through E Corp and their products, which infiltrate people's lives to the point of their dependence on them. Power is in the act of hacking anonymously that causes social disruption. Power is in the surveillance that anyone can perform. Power is what makes you feel like you're being watched. Power is in the health industry and in the way our body interacts with the world. Power is an operation and a relation that permeates our lives and the social institutions we rely on in immeasurable ways. Power itself doesn't really exist independently of these processes. So long as we are in a disciplinary regime, power isn't something that anyone can possess.

So, is Price worried about Mr. Robot having more power than he does? Is he worried about Angela or Zheng? If Foucault is right, it doesn't matter. Phillip Price will never be the most powerful person in the room. And neither will anyone else.

III

They All Think I'm the Ringleader

7
What Kind of Revolutionary Is Mr. Robot?

SHANE J. RALSTON

Besides being the title of an EP by *The (International) Noise Conspiracy*, "Bigger cages, longer chains!" is an anarchist rallying cry. It's meant to ridicule those political activists who compromise their ideals, make demands and then settle for partial concessions or, to put it bluntly, bargain with the Man.

In *Mr. Robot*, Christian Slater plays the anarchist leader of a hacktivist group known as fsociety. Mr. Robot won't negotiate with the FBI and E(vil) Corp for bigger cages and longer chains. He tells Elliot Anderson, the young cybersecurity expert and hacker, "We live in a kingdom of bullshit!" Victory over the tyranny of corporations and states requires radical means to achieve radical ends. Mr. Robot wants freedom without limits, total liberation from corporate and statist control, and the opportunity to live in a world without bullshit. Mr. Robot's objective is to free citizens of first-world nations from the cages of consumer debt and citizens of third-world nations from the shackles of extreme poverty. Meeting half-way will not do.

Where did these ideas come from? What are the inspirations for Mr. Robot's hacktivist philosophy? The most obvious sources are David Graeber's anarchism, which also influenced the Occupy Wall Street movement, and the hacktivist group Anonymous's *moralfaggery*—the policy of some of its members to use collective computer hacking to serve the greater good.

Candidates for more remote sources are Marxism and pragmatism; the former, a blueprint for freeing the working class from their bourgeois oppressors; the latter, a philosophy of action, intelligent inquiry and democratic reform. Some might object that pragmatism is too conventional to be compatible with the radical ideas that motivate Mr. Robot's worldview. Hacktivism demands action, not mere thinking! But any organized social-political movement requires a well-thought-out plan as well as a vision of what its participants hope to achieve. Since pragmatism is a philosophy of action and reform, it's possible that Mr. Robot is a closet pragmatist!

Graeber and Occupy Wall Street

On September 17th 2011, nearly four hundred people flooded into Zuccotti Park in New York's Wall Street district to engage in political protest. They expressed frustration at the recent government bailout of big banks after the financial crisis, growing income inequality, powerlessness of the US electorate, political corruption and escalating consumer debt in the corporate-dominated American economy.

Two hundred activists stayed overnight in the park, setting up a tent city with amenities for sustaining a long-term camp-in. As time went on, the movement gained traction and support grew among the young and old, including members of the US Communist Party, Greenpeace, House Democratic Leader representative Nancy Pelosi, labor unions and some celebrities too. Political jokester Jon Stewart even showed solidarity with the Occupy activists: "If the people who were supposed to fix our financial system had actually done it, the people who have no idea how to solve these problems wouldn't be getting shit for not offering solutions" (*The Daily Show*, October 7th). Things had gotten out of hand. And they only looked to be getting worse. It was time for the Ninety-Nine Percent, as they called themselves, to tell the remaining one percent of the population, the political and economic elites, that enough is enough!

One of the masterminds behind Occupy Wall Street was a man named David Graeber, an anthropologist, anarchist, and activist who became disillusioned with the establishment after a decade teaching at Yale University. Once he got into political hot water with the university administration, Yale refused to rehire him. One of his last seminars, titled "Direct Action and Radical Social Theory," signaled his transition from academic to activist.

In 2011, Graeber attended the initial organizing committee for Occupy Wall Street, but was convinced that they would only negotiate for bigger cages and longer chains. So he formed his own committee of leaderless, anti-authoritarian, anti-corporate hooligans who spearheaded the Occupy protest with inspiration from classic anarchism. Although more of an intellectual than Mr. Robot, Graeber would likely agree with him that consumer debt must end. In an interview about his sixth book, *Debt: The First 5000 Years*, Graeber laments:

> The money has to be extracted from the most vulnerable members of society. Lives are destroyed; millions of people die. People would never dream of supporting such a policy until you say, "Well, they have to pay their debts."

Anonymous and Moralfaggery

Besides Graeber and Occupy Wall Street, another philosophical inspiration for Mr. Robot's hacktivism is the activist network Anonymous and the agenda of some of their members, called *moralfaggery*. Wearing Guy Fawkes masks at physical protests and bombarding servers in collective cyber-attacks, Anonymous harassed the Church of Scientology, PayPal, MasterCard, Visa, Sony, as well as the governments of the US, Israel, Tunisia, and Uganada.

The term *moralfag* describes hackers in the Anonymous network who commit themselves to their craft not just for the fun of it or to piss someone off, but for a higher cause, such as defending human rights or liberating humankind. Likewise, Mr. Robot sees the defeat of E(vil) Corp and freeing people from the shackles of consumer debt and poverty as a higher calling. He is not just hacking because it's a titillating activity or trolling to anger the Man. In the vernacular of Anonymous, Mr. Robot is a *moralfag*.

Anonymous's attack on the Church of Scientology bears a shocking resemblance to Mr. Robot's cyber-attack on E(vil) Corp. In 2008, Anonymous started its campaign against Scientology by ridiculing Tom Cruise's Church-sponsored video interview. After receiving a cease-and-desist letter from Church attorneys, Anonymous's network of hacktivists engaged in a guerrilla war of retaliatory measures, including prank calls, cyber-hacks on its websites and even sending blacked-out faxes to exhaust the Church's printer ink cartridges. A writer at *The Economist* describes the organization of Anonymous's hacktivist campaign against Scientology:

> Organised from a Wikipedia-style website (editable by anyone) and through anonymous internet chat rooms, "Project Chanology," as the initiative is known, presents no easy target for Scientology's lawyers. ("Fair Game")

Although Anonymous didn't frame a Church executive, as Elliot did under the tutelage of Mr. Robot, they used almost every *fsociety* tactic in their fight against the wealthy Church of Scientology. The Anonymous network cyber-hacks included Distributed Denial of Service (DDoS) attacks, where hacktivists crashed online services by overwhelming them with requests, and the Low Orbit Ion Cannon (LOIC), where traffic from many sources was used to overrun servers. The Anonymous campaign escalated into real-world protests at Church of Scientology locations around the globe. Hacktivists donned Guy Fawkes masks and carried signs reading "Down with This Sort of Thing" and "Scientology Destroys Lives."

After the FBI arrested and jailed some members for the Church cyber-attacks, a period of in-fighting occurred within

Anonymous. It gave rise to two factions: *moralfags*, who hack for a higher purpose or calling, and *trolls*, who hack for the fun of it or to upset others. Of course, Mr. Robot is a *moralfag*, not a troll.

Dewey, Trotsky and the Means-End Continuum

It's easy to find contemporary inspirations for the Mr. Robot character. He's like Occupy Wall Street's David Graeber or Anonymous's *moralfags*. But what are some historical sources for Mr. Robot's hacktivist philosophy? The Russian Marxist revolutionary Leon Trotsky (1879–1940) and the American pragmatist philosopher John Dewey (1859–1952) had an intense debate in the 1920s about which of their philosophies is better suited for sorting out the proper relationship between means and ends. The question of whether the end justifies any means is a recurring dispute among political operatives and activists (as well as hacktivists)—some who are more principled, while others who are, let's say, more diabolical.

Take, for instance, the 2016 American presidential election, when former hacktivist-turned-whistleblower Julian Assange, founder of Wikileaks, published e-mails of former Secretary-of-State-turned-Democratic-presidential-candidate Hillary Clinton. To defeat an authoritarian, misogynistic, fear-mongering figure like Republican presidential candidate Donald Trump, the Democratic Party recruited Malcolm Nance, an ex-intelligence-official-turned-politico, to tell the public that the Wikileaks documents were fakes supplied by Russian president Vladimir Putin. However, the story did not track the truth. Wikileaks had a perfect record of producing authentic documents. The Kremlin denied collaborating with Assange or Wikileaks. In other words, Nance was spreading lies. Sometimes the end (in this case, winning an election) will justify even the most morally objectionable means (such as telling bald-faced lies).

Compared to Dewey the mild-mannered professor, Leon Trotsky was a divisive figure with a colorful past. Along with

Vladimir Lenin, he planned and led the successful assault on the Winter Palace in the Bolshevist-Russian Revolution of October 1917. Trotsky also served as the War Commissar for the Red Army in its drive to rid Russia of foreign-supported Tsarist forces during its bloody civil war. In an essay entitled "Their Morals and Ours," he articulated a Marxist vision of morality that departed from all other ethical systems. For Trotsky, doing the right thing does not require obedience to divine commands, universal laws or imperatives of reason. Instead, the capital owning class (or bourgeoisie) uses its "petty bourgeois morality" to hypnotize the working class (or proletariat) into a state of compliant obedience—what Marxists call "false consciousness." Trotsky insisted that the only ethical system that truly benefits the proletariat is the one that recommends violent revolutionary action in the service of "liberating mankind" (*Their Morals and Ours*).

John Dewey disagreed. In the essay "Means and Ends," he argued that even an ethically defensible end cannot justify the selection of *any* means whatsoever. The liberation of humankind—which Dewey commended Trotsky for adopting—requires democratic and experimental means for its realization. According to Dewey, the first step in navigating the means-end continuum is to survey

> all means that are likely to attain this end without any fixed preoccupation as to what they must be, and that every suggested means would be weighed and judged on the express ground of the consequences it is likely to produce.

The problem with Trotsky's approach is that class struggle becomes *the* exclusive method to liberate humankind. It then licenses all ancillary means, including murder and torture, to achieve that vaunted end. As I have argued in *Great Debates Reconstructed*, Marxist ethics, while adversarial and revolutionary, was insufficiently democratic and experimental for Dewey's tastes.

Trotsky clung to the absolutist doctrine of Marxism even when alternatives to class struggle would have proven more effective. He wrote the essay "Their Morals and Ours" as a response to the widespread criticism of his handling of the Kronstadt rebellion, an uprising of sailors in the Russian port city of Kronstadt during the Russian civil war. In March of 1921, near the end of the war, the Trotsky-led Red Army brutally suppressed the Kronstadt labor strike. According to Trotsky's biographer, "He would not have written it if not for the fact that at the time he had come under attack over his position and actions, seventeen years earlier, during the Kronstadt rebellion." The protest was organized to demonstrate the workers' discontent over low wages and poor working conditions. Even though the strike reflected the ideals of the Russian Revolution, it stood in the way of Trotsky achieving his strategic goals. "Problems of revolutionary morality," Trotsky wrote, "are fused with the problems of revolutionary strategy and tactics." According to Trotsky's playbook, it was acceptable to act on the ethical principle that the end justifies using any means whatsoever to obtain it, no matter how brutal or contrary to the revolutionary movement's ideals.

Mr. Robot is not a Marxist, at least not one in the mold of Leon Trotsky. In the first episode of Season 1.0 he pressures Elliot to give him the DAT file so that fsociety can insert a rootkit into E(vil) Corp's server. Once inserted, the outcome will be two-fold: 1. secure a load of data and e-mails that fsociety can later threaten to dump into the public domain and 2. leave a trail of false evidence pointing to E(vil) Corp's Chief Technology Officer as the hack's culprit. "Once you do that," Mr. Robot tells Elliot, "we will have put in motion the biggest revolution that the world has ever seen."

While he employs the Marxist language of revolution, other jargon such as *class struggle, historical dialectic, false consciousness* and *Communist utopia* never fall from Mr. Robot's lips. He also doesn't rely on Trotsky's playbook. He appreciates hacking as the most effective means for reaching his final goal, but the goal does not justify selecting any methods whatsoever, no matter how unsavory. For instance, replacing debt slavery with actual slavery would not be an acceptable means, for it would undermine the ideals of the movement. Instead, Mr. Robot hand-picks those means that will achieve his end-in-view while preserving the fsociety movement's integrity. What Dewey, Trotsky and Mr. Robot all share in common is a single overarching objective: liberating humankind.

Mr. Robot—Anarchist or Pragmatist?

In the second episode Mr. Robot presses Elliot to frame the E(vil) Corp executive Terry Colby for the hack, declaring, "You are either a one or a zero! You are either going to act or not!" This propensity toward action points in the direction of pragmatism, but the overall objective of the action—to free the world from corporate control and domination—has its roots in anarchism. It could be said that Mr. Robot's means are pragmatist while his ends are anarchist. Dewey's insight is that the means chosen should always be suited to achieve the end. Dewey recommends democratic means to achieve democratic ends. But Mr. Robot's ends are anarchist. Thus, they require anarchist means.

Anarchist means include subversion, violence and even harassment, all of which would probably not pass democratic muster. The qualification *probably* is important here. Sometimes violence can constitute a democratic means. For Dewey, democratic methods usually encompass careful inquiry, organization, intelligence and experimentation. Yet he also noted an exceptional case:

> The one exception—and that apparent rather than real—to dependence upon organized intelligence is found when society through an authorized majority has entered upon a path of social experimentation leading to great social change, and a minority refuses by force to permit the intelligent action to go into effect. Then force may be intelligently employed to subdue and disarm the recalcitrant minority. (*Liberalism and Social Action*)

Violent action may be undertaken against a "recalcitrant minority" if the minority refuses to conform to the will of a democratic majority. If the minority is one percent of the population, or the social and economic elites, then it would seem that, according to the logic of Dewey (as well as some anarchists in the Occupy movement), the Ninety-Nine Percent are justified in forcing the elites to comply with an agenda of social, economic, and political reform.

So the answer to the question of whether Mr. Robot's hacktivist philosophy is anarchist or pragmatist is not so simple. Mr. Robot's identity is not so simple either. By the end of Season 1.0 it is revealed that Mr. Robot is one of Elliot's multiple (well, at least two that we know of) personalities, a dominant force in the main character's split psyche. Elliot's Mr. Robot persona impels him to bring his hacking to a higher level, from prying into the lives of those around him to liberating the world from corporate domination—or in the vernacular of Anonymous, from trolling to *moralfaggery*.

Less Thinking, More Action!

Karl Marx wrote that the point of Communism is to change the world, not to philosophize about it. Even though Mr. Robot isn't a Marxist, he can still appreciate what happens when you have too much philosophizing, not enough action. The danger is that the window of opportunity to act and change the world will pass. It might even mean settling for bigger cages and longer chains. Armchair philosophers might not like all this talk of action. However, if a philosopher is to become an activist (sometimes they are called 'public philosophers'), then she has to combine theory with action. Ideas can change the world, but it takes bodies and force if you want to make it happen now.

The advantage of Mr. Robot's hacktivist philosophy is that it entertains just the right mix of action and philosophy (including anarchism and pragmatism); enough to motivate effective activism (or hacktivism), but not so much as to induce cerebral overload or idle slumber (think of the effect of a boring philosophy lecture). So, is Mr. Robot a closet pragmatist? Probably. His hacktivism is predominantly anarchist, but with a pinch of the pragmatic thrown in for good measure. Shouldn't the best social-political movements, like the tastiest mixed drinks, contain a combination of spirits?

8
Mr. Robot, Mad Son of *Noir*

CHRISTOPHER HOYT

Mr. *Robot* is a *neo-noir* thriller for our time, and by examining its place within the tradition of *film noir* we can see ourselves, and the central philosophical problems of our age, more clearly.

The loosely-bound genre known as *film noir* originated in America around World War II, and ever since then it has been a powerful and popular means of engaging a number of pressing, existential questions. The most important and most potent of those question is this: How is an individual to live a life of integrity in a world devoid of truth, justice, and absolute meaning?

In the earliest days of *film noir*, the heroes were laconic, brooding types who faced the abyss with cynical machismo. "The worst that can happen to me is that I get killed," those classic noir heroes seem to be saying, "and so what, we all have to die." By 2015, we get *Mr. Robot*, in which all of our central characters seem to be undergoing mental breakdowns under the stress of modern life. How did we get here?

Before There Was Fortran

To answer that question, it will help to start still further back in time, around the turn of the last century. It's almost impossible to imagine now, but at that point in history,

Western civilization was gripped by a spirit of optimism unlike anything before or since. There were plenty of problems and cynics, of course, but the dominant mood was one of profound hopefulness.

The machine age was then about a century underway, and science and technology were beginning to make profound changes in the lives of the masses. Skyscrapers, elevators, automobiles, radio, airplanes, tractors, and movies were all new. The phonograph, electricity, electric lights, and washing machines, were too. Trains had been around only a half-century or so, and both trolleys and subways were newer still. The Eiffel Tower, the grandest homage to industry the world has ever known, opened at the World's Fair of 1889, and the first really big steel Ferris Wheel was erected four years later in Chicago, at the World's Columbian Exhibition.

Mass-produced china and flatware, vaccines for typhoid and plague, aspirin and x-rays all seemed to foretoken a coming age of prosperity. In short, to the majority, science and technology appeared to promise a wealth of almost incomprehensible benefits for the common man as well as the prince. This mood was captured by H.G. Wells in *A Modern Utopia*, first published in 1905, which envisioned an egalitarian world where technology met humanity's needs so fully that physical labor, exploitation, and most misery were simply eliminated.

The spell was broken in 1914 when World War I erupted and civilization had to face the reality that plenty does not guarantee peace, and the reality that technology had only exaggerated the reach and power of injustice, pollution, destruction, and suffering. Those optimists who managed to raise their spirits in the Roaring Twenties, after the Great War, confronted not only the profound class inequality of that time, but soon enough the shocks of the Great Depression and World War II. The halcyon days were gone, and the West was in a funk.

For a lot of people, the monumental suffering of innocents also proved Nietzsche's point that "God is dead," that is, the West had changed politically and epistemologically in ways that displaced all ideas about absolute truth and morality. Man seemed to be master of his own fate, and he had proved to be a master with a depressing capacity for wretchedness. It was then, during World War II, that *film noir* was born, an American art form expressing a nihilistic outlook. There is no absolute truth, no guarantee of justice, no happy ending you can count on, kid, and you just have to keep going anyway. These same messages were central to existentialism, the philosophical movement that emerged in France at the same time. In both, there is an emphasis on the fact that you must live and define yourself in a world that lacks any intrinsic sense of purpose. Your choices define you, but you must choose in a context that is murky all the way down.

So, *film noir* was born in the cauldron of mid-twentieth century disappointment and cynicism brought on by the great historical traumas of that era. The term *"film noir,"* which means "black film" or "somber film," was coined by the French critic Nino Frank in 1946, and the name stuck. What happened was that during World War II, a style of filmmaking evolved in America that was much more somber and cynical than what had existed in Hollywood in the 1920s and 1930s.

Frank and his fellow Europeans didn't get a chance to see the newer work until the war was over because of Nazi embargoes, and when they did, they were stunned. The chipper musicals and morally certain westerns Nino and his contemporaries had known were nothing like such dark, complicated *noir* thrillers as *Stranger on the Third Floor* (1940) or *The Maltese Falcon* (1941). In these newer films, the heroes were morally compromised, the good guys often died, and the villains were nearly all sympathetic characters, sometimes even more than the heroes. The war-time films depicted a world of moral ambiguity and epistemological uncertainty that was new and startling in its day. The black-and-white *noir* films made between 1940 and 1958 are now referred to as "classic noir," while films produced after 1960 are now called "neo-noir."

Men in Filthy White Hats

In classic *noir* films, the task of the hero is typically to navigate our morally complicated world without losing his integrity entirely, though he is nearly always compromised and complicated himself. For example, consider Sam Spade, the hero of *The Maltese Falcon*, who is a pretty unsavory character. Early in the movie, we learn that Spade has been having an affair with his partner's wife even though he doesn't even like her and treats her with deep disrespect. And when his partner, Miles Archer, is murdered, Spade couldn't care less. However, very near the end of the movie, Spade chooses to turn his girlfriend, Brigid, over to the police, and he explains his reasoning in a long, powerful monologue. Spade is brilliantly played by Humphrey Bogart, who stares into the distance with almost lunatic intensity, while he explains to Brigid—and to himself, really—his decision. "Maybe I do love you," he tells her," I'll have some rotten nights after I've sent you over, but that'll pass." Then he continues:

> When a man's partner is killed, he's supposed to do something about it. It doesn't make any difference what you thought of him. He was your partner and you're supposed to do something about it.

If he doesn't turn Brigid in, Spade will be just another corrupt private eye, a man with no integrity in a world without integrity, a self-serving villain in a world of self-serving villains, and Spade painfully chooses instead an identity he can live with. This existential task of self-definition in a world that threatens to corrupt us is a constant refrain of *film noir.*

Rami Malek, the star of *Mr. Robot*, has a good deal in common with Bogart. Bogart's great talent was to portray men who were cynical and macho enough to navigate the criminal world's they entered, yet vulnerable enough for us to identify with them and to care about them. Bogart's physical presence had a lot to do with his appeal. He was decidedly slight, not especially handsome, spoke in a peculiar croak, and his pensive eyes nearly always seemed just a little sad beneath his perpetually wrinkled brow. The effect was to represent an everyday man making his way through an unpredictable world by remaining lonely, aloof, and skeptical.

Malek is better looking than Bogart and in better shape, but he, too, is unquestionably slight compared to the drug dealers, convicts, federal agents, and corporate goons that his character boldly faces down. And even more so than Bogart, Malek's most distinctive feature is certainly his enormous, pensive eyes. Malek's eyes are startlingly big, and the way they are lit by the show's cinematographer, Tod Campbell, they nearly always seem to express an exaggerated, fearful attentiveness. Like Bogart, he is our guide to the dark corners of our world, but Malek's Elliot doesn't project Bogart's sad cynicism, but a decidedly more fearful, troubled mood.

To see my point, it might help to compare two scenes, one from *The Big Sleep* (1946) and one from *Mr. Robot*. In *The Big Sleep*, Bogart again plays a private detective, this time Philip Marlowe, who is up against an outfit of gangsters guilty of gambling, pornography, murder, and other old-school crimes. In one scene, Marlowe visits a casino run by his nemesis, Eddie Mars, located in what appears to be an upper-middle class suburban home. The casino is filled with well-off patrons dressed as if for an opera, and Bogart is invited to check his coat at the door, as you would at a posh restaurant. Inside the casino, Marlowe smiles approvingly while his love interest, Vivienne, accompanied by a band dressed in blazers and bow ties, cheerfully sings "And Her Tears Flowed Like Wine," a chipper little ditty with lines like these:

And when his wife said, "Hey now!
What did you get for me?"
He socked her in the chopper,
Such a sweet, sweet guy was he!
And her tears flowed like wine.

The message is clear: the veneer of polite society is paper thin, and what lies below is pretty ugly. Marlowe makes it through with his winning combination of grace, a gun in his coat pocket, and that sardonic sneer of Bogart's that lets us know he's not fooled for a minute.

An analogous scene from *Mr. Robot* occurs just a few minutes into the first episode when Elliot confronts Rohit D'Temeta, a child pornographer who presents himself as a polite, well-dressed coffee shop owner. Like Spade, Elliot is our guide to the depravities of the modern world, an everyman who has mastered D'Temeta's realm of digital wickedness. But unlike Marlowe, Elliot's protection isn't weary doubt, but rather this: When D'Temeta offers to buy him off, Elliot responds, "That's the part you were wrong about, Rohit. I don't give a shit about money." Whereas Bogart's characters shield their integrity behind sad skepticism, Elliot exudes the power of the modern whiz-kid, an alienated teenager's disdain for money, authority, and conventional recognition. He is the new Bogart, the new everyman who can see the truths that lie beneath the veneer of polite society, but those truths are hidden in the digital realm and Elliot's weapons are computers and smartphones, not guns.

It is a striking fact that Elliot comes across as so juvenile, in contrast to Spade, Marlowe, and other classic *noir* heroes. Some of this is due to age, of course; Bogart was forty-two when *The Maltese Falcon* was filmed, Malek thirty-three during the first season of *Mr. Robot*. However, thirty-three is hardly a boy, and were he cast in 1941, Malek would have had to man up. The characters' costumes are certainly relevant here: Elliot wears hoodies and Chuck Taylors, and he carries a backpack with a laptop in it. Spade wears suits and fedoras, and he carries a gun. Still more is conveyed by the actors' body language: at his office, Malek slouches and demurs like a child forced to go to church, while Bogart always has the bearing of a confident war veteran. The effect of Elliot's juvenile characteristics is to drive home the point that the adult world—the world of corporations and government, the world of money and careers—must be forsaken if Elliot is to guard his integrity. Teenagers, free as they are from car payments, mortgages, and children of their own, can still afford to pass up the devilish deals offered us in our modern, capitalist society.

Classic *noir* was visually characterized by dark shadows, broken lines, and cockeyed framing that gave visual form to the moral and epistemological ambiguities it thematized. The style of classic *noir* leaves the viewer feeling uneasy and uncertain, just as the characters in them feel. Neo-*noir* movies like *Fight Club* and *The Matrix* use many visual techniques to create the uncomfortable settings their heroes operate in, one of the most important of which is their careful use of color, the colors they accent in production as well as in design. In neo-*noir* films, offices are typically places of extreme alienation, places that most deeply threaten the characters' authenticity. Row upon row of gray cubicles and beige copiers are lit in the sickly-greens of exaggerated fluorescent lights, a palette that not coincidentally makes the people look sallow and glum.

Here is an important point at which *Mr. Robot* has something really new to say. In *Mr. Robot*, the offices are shot in a harsh blue-gray that doesn't leave you feeling quite sick, but rather just awfully cold. The offices in *Mr. Robot* are, in fact, quite pretty, and clearly convey wealth and power, yet they are still severe and sterile. What should we make of this update to the neo-*noir* style? I think it reflects a growing anxiety about the fact that we are tempted by these spaces, by their prestige and their futuristic chic. Elliot's own apartment is shot in warmer palette of earth tones, it feels human and familiar, at least to those of us who have rented city apartments on a budget, but it's also a dump, and, like Elliot's clothes, it looks like a teenager's space.

Despite that he's a star in a lucrative field, Elliot has decorated his apartment like a college crash pad with thrift-store furniture and band posters. The effect, I believe, is that you can only feel so bad about the office and so good about the apartment. We're in a modern-day quandary here: we know that money is a trap, but what's the alternative?

Phillip Price's office and Angela Moss's Season Two apartment are formulaic and cold, but they are very pretty, luxurious, and far nicer than what most of us in the audience have. The traps of money, power, and luxury are hard to escape.

Campbell (the cinematographer) often employs a relatively uncommon framing technique called "shortsighting," in which the character is positioned towards the edge of the frame and faces out, not in, leaving little distance between his eyes and the edge of the frame. In shot after shot, we see characters posed with a lot of space around them but no other visible characters. They are alone, and we feel their isolation. Classic *noir* and *neo-noir* commonly frame individual characters as well, but they are either centered in the frame or looking across it, and the effect on us, the viewers, is quite different.

In that scene from *The Maltese Falcon* that I described earlier, the one in which Bogart contemplates his choice to turn his girlfriend over to the police, the frame is filled with a crooked close-up of Bogart's tormented face. He is alone with this choice, and alone on the screen. However, the way Campbell shortsights Elliot, Angela, Darlene, Tyrell and other characters in *Mr. Robot* emphasizes not just that they are alone with their choices, but also that unknown threats lie, or might lie, uncomfortably close by. In these moments, the characters in *Mr. Robot* seem pressed to make existential decisions under particular duress, in a world that seems to be closing in on them.

Bogart appears deeply pained, but sure of himself nonetheless. By contrast, Malek often looks frightened and uncertain. It's always tough to face our existential responsibility for our choices, but in *Mr. Robot,* there seems to be no space the characters can retreat to make their choices in peace.

You Can't Beat the System

We're beginning to narrow in on an answer to the question with which we began: the characters in *Mr. Robot* are losing their minds because the threats to personal integrity are so profound and so pervasive that they're breaking under the pressure. But we're only just beginning to answer the question, since it might sound like I'm saying only that money and power corrupt.

To get a more satisfying answer, we have to look more seriously at the political messages of the show, and here again it helps to locate *Mr. Robot* within the history of *film noir*. The villains in classic *noir* were mostly old-fashioned gangsters who robbed banks and stole diamonds and such, and the classic hero was the private detective who faced them down. Classic *noir* died out in 1958, as the red scare and a new wave of American conservatism squeezed *noir* doubts out of the mainstream. Some great *neo-noir* movies were made in the 1960s, but the style really came into its own in the 1970s, in the wake of Payola, the Viet Nam War, Watergate, the Cuyahoga River in Cleveland catching on fire, and other scandals. It was then that the doubts and distrust of *film noir*, first born in the horrors of World War II, repopulated the public imagination.

Whereas in classic *noir* the hero was threatened by a world without inherent meaning, *neo-noir* often points a finger of blame at capitalism, commercialism, and corrupt leadership. In the celebrated *neo-noir*, *Chinatown*, private detective Jake Gittes discovers a conspiracy of government officials and wealthy elites who have plotted to bankrupt the farmers of Owens County, California by diverting their water supply, then buying up the land before turning the water back on. The movie, which was based on true events (!), ends with Gittes's failure; the conspiracy is too far-reaching, too powerful, and too amorphous to stop.

The anxiety about powerful conspiracies expressed in *Chinatown* reached new heights after 9/11, bringing us up to the present. Consider *Quantum of Solace* (2008), a mediocre movie by most measures but a truly remarkable cultural artifact. Since his debut in *Dr. No* (1962), James Bond was the epitome of composure, a character who could drink martinis all night long without even getting tipsy, a hero who would protect the good and dispatch the bad! But in *Quantum of Solace*, for the first time, James Bond is drunk, disheveled, and nearly broken. Exactly like *Chinatown*, the plot of *Quantum of Solace* centers on a conspiracy to divert water from poor farmers, but this time, the conspiracy is global, not American, and it involves not only financial elites, but also the CIA, MI6, and the highest officials in the US and British governments.

Bond is breaking under the weight of a world so corrupt that he might not be able to fix it, and he's got no guarantee that M and her pals will ever trust him again. He might be the last sane man in an insane world, but suddenly Bond isn't so sure about anything. But hey, it's a Bond film, and it ends with hope, redemption, and an opening for sequels.

We don't know the outcome of fsociety's anarchic revolution yet, but we do know that the conspiracy they are up against may well be unbeatable. There's a telling scene in the episode "eps2.7_init_5.fve" in which Price, the CEO of Evil Corp, meets with Zhang, the Chinese Minister of State Security, whom we know to be Whiterose, the head of a violent and dangerous gang of Chinese hackers. The two men are negotiating, and it's clear that Price was to arrange for a power plant in New Jersey to come under Chinese control.

> PRICE: As of noon this Friday, I'm sorry to say, the Washington Township plant will be taken over by the federal government.

> ZHANG: And here I thought we were taking a step forward, but here we stand two steps back.

As the scene plays out, it's clear that Zhang assumes that Price—the CEO of a private company—has arranged the federal takeover, and that Price could prevent it if he tried. Zhang simply assumes that Price can control federal actions—and many events in *Mr. Robot* suggest that Zhang is right. In a world this corrupt, what hope does a quasi-adolescent hacker from New York really have? It's no wonder he's breaking. Bond drinks too much Scotch and struggles to maintain his cool, and Elliot retreats into morphine and full-blown insanity.

Mr. Robot wastes no time getting into the crazy-making state of corruption in our modern world. The first minute of the first episode of the first season begin in the fashion of many great *films noir:* with a voiceover that invites us into the private thoughts of the hero. But these thoughts are pretty wacko. "Hello Friend," says Elliot to us while we look at a blank screen. The voice is especially intimate, the microphone so close that Malek is just this side of whispering, his voice pitched at the volume of lover lying next to us in a quiet bed. But within just a few lines, the voiceover takes an odd turn: "You're only in my head," Elliot says quietly into our ears, "I'm talking to an imaginary person." Quickly, the monologue changes direction yet again, but this turn is into still more madness:

> What I'm about to tell you is top secret. A conspiracy bigger than all of us. There's a powerful group of people out there that are secretly running the world.

A "top secret" global conspiracy of elites who secretly rule the world? Does this guy wear a tinfoil hat? And yet . . . an awful lot of people nowadays believe that there is such a conspiracy. Donald Trump's surprising election was fueled in large part by his status as an outsider and his promise to "drain the swamp" of corrupt elites. What Trump will actually do remains to be seen, but a lot of people on both the left and the right are pretty sure he's right—that politicians and billionaires do in fact conspire to rewrite laws, influence public opinion, and manipulate events of global significance simply to serve their own interests. The mainstreaming of ostensibly paranoid anxieties is an important sign of the times.

Sam Esmail has said that a chief source of inspiration for *Mr. Robot* was *Fight Club*, the 1999 David Fincher *neo-noir* picture about another anarchist collective, Project Mayhem, which, like fsociety, is committed to a violent rebellion against crony capitalism. In *Fight Club*, as in *Mr. Robot,* the narrator loses his mind in his fight against the world. Like Elliot, the nameless narrator of *Fight Club* suffers what

93

psychologists call "dissociative identity disorder," a condition in which the mind fragments and the core self attributes certain of its own thoughts, feelings, and actions to another person or persons. Modern life is just too much for him.

Similarly, in *American Psycho* (2000), yet another movie that anticipates *Mr. Robot* and *neo-noir* insanity, Patrick Bateman goes on a killing spree to vent his anger and disgust at the outrageously superficial world of 1980s Wall Street. He's disgusted with himself and angry at the world that made him the superficial, hollow man that he is. Like Project Mayhem and fsociety, Bateman strikes out violently. However, Bateman's salvation is purely personal, not political. He has no notion of changing the system, but only of lashing out. Project Mayhem does some real damage to Wall Street by the end of the movie, but it still looks mostly like anarchic vengeance, not a political revolution.

Mr. Robot is different. fsociety may not have a well-designed plan for the future, but they are engaged in revolution, not merely personal venting. Indeed, in Season Two the characters struggle to know whether they've done the right thing by attacking Evil Corp. We in the audience are stuck wondering not just if the demise of Evil Corp was worth all the human suffering it caused, but also whether fsociety is being played by Zhang, by Price, or by both.

Mr. Robot raises these questions, but it certainly doesn't answer them—or, not yet, anyway. It's crazy enough to talk about a global conspiracy of elites, let alone to imagine that a kid in a hoodie and Chuck Taylors can outmaneuver the most powerful people on Earth. But then again, Trump got elected, and you might just want to drain the stinking swamp and see what happens.

Or will President Trump merely drain that swamp into his own cabinet and rule over the conspiracy of elites from the White House? Man, it's complicated. You might go nuts if you think about this stuff too much.

9
What Elliot Doesn't Know Won't Hurt You (Or Will It?)

RICHARD GREENE

Perhaps the greatest irony of *Mr. Robot* is that Elliot Alderson, the show's protagonist, uses things he knows to exact revenge on folks that harm or threaten him, to bring wrong doers to justice, and to bring about a complete re-ordering of the world's financial structure by destroying the records of the world's largest credit corporation— E Corp.

For example, the very first episode begins with Elliot confronting a man in a coffee shop. Elliot has hacked into this man's computer and determined that he is the leader of a child pornography ring. The man assumes (as does the audience momentarily) that Elliot is shaking him down, but then the police come in, and arrest the man. Elliot is using his knowledge, which he attains by employing his world-class hacker skills, for good. He is a hero who fights for justice.

The irony, of course, lies in the fact that Elliot is in about the worst position to *know* things as you could ever hope to find yourself. He's virtually chock-a-block with personal skeptical scenarios, each of which conspire against him in his attempts to be certain of even the most mundane of facts. This raises the question, what, if anything, does Elliot know?

A Very Brief History of Skepticism

Philosophical skepticism, as opposed to the sort of skepticism that conspiracy theorists employ, is a skepticism about our knowledge. Whereas conspiracy theorists don't deny that knowledge, in general, is possible; rather, they just believe that someone is lying to them or misleading them or some such, about some particular thing. Philosophical skeptics, on the other hand, believe that knowledge in some cases—usually cases where we're normally inclined to think that we have knowledge—is systematically ruled out.

So the conspiracy theorist, for example, might hold that E Corp is deceiving folks about the future of the stock market in order to affect interest rates in a way that is to E Corp's own benefit. Conspiracy theories and conspiracy theorists are many and manifold. In fact, if *Mr. Robot* weren't a work of fiction, I have little doubt that there would be a whole slew of fsociety deniers—folks that believe that the fall of E Corp didn't actually happen (nowadays they would deem the report of E Corp's collapse as fake news). In contrast, the philosophical skeptic, of whom there are few, might argue that knowledge of E Corp, the stock market, interest rates, the external world, and Tyrell Wellick are not possible.

One way of thinking about the difference is that the conspiracy theorist skeptic asserts that some of the things that most people think are true are really false, but the philosophical skeptic doesn't go that far: they maintain that one just can't know about certain things (the right thing to do is to suspend judgment about such matters).

The history of philosophy is bursting with great skeptical scenarios. Philosophical skepticism dates back to around the ninth century B.C.E., when early Indian philosophers, began to cast doubt on the possibility of philosophical knowledge, but the sort of skepticism we're interested in—skepticism about the existence of the world around us—begins in the seventeenth century when René Descartes wrote his *Meditations on First Philosophy*.

Descartes raised a number of skeptical scenarios, all designed to cast doubt on our beliefs about the external world. He considered that his apparent experiences of the world might be based on faulty senses, which could possibly be the result of his being mad. He also considered that everything he's experiencing might be a dream. Finally, he considered that his experiences might all arise from some source that is not reliable (in Descartes's case it was the handiwork of an evil demon—a being as powerful as God, but only interested in deception). We'll see how these apply to Elliot, but first let's see how they work.

The key to a really good skeptical argument is you have to have a good skeptical hypothesis. A skeptical hypothesis is a story that explains why you have the experiences that you have, but also explains why your experiences don't accurately represent the way the world is. One such story might go as follows. Suppose that Elliot decides to go to Atlantic City to catch a hypnotist show, and winds up on stage. Presumably the hypnotist could make him believe that just about anything is true. For example, the hypnotist could make him believe that he is on Coney Island at fsociety headquarters when, in fact, he is onstage in Atlantic City. He could make him think that he is talking to Darlene, his sister, when in fact he is talking to Nucky Thompson.[1] He could make him think that there is an Evil Corporation that needs to be destroyed, when, in reality, E Corp is a fledgling online banking company, to which the hypnotist happens to owe a few thousand dollars.

To see how skepticism works, we don't actually need Elliot to have gone to the hypnotist show in Atlantic City. It's just enough to note that it could be the case that Elliot could have done so, and that he can't rule out the possibility that he went to the show.

---

[1] If you don't know who Nucky Thompson is, you'll want to run out and purchase a copy of *Boardwalk Empire and Philosophy*. This may look like a shameless plug, but if you've been following the discussion to this point, you can't be so sure of that, can you?

Elliot doesn't remember going to Atlantic City, but the hypnotist could have made him forget that he had—we're talking about a really good hypnotist here. You're no doubt thinking "But no hypnotist is that good." Yet, if a really good hypnotist wanted you to fix his financial situation, it would be smart of him or her to trick you into thinking that hypnotists lack the skills to do such things. Just sayin' . . . So, for pretty much anything Elliot is thinking about the way the world is, he's not in a position to rule out that some hypnotist tricked him to thinking that's the way the world is.

By the way, dear reader, this applies to you, too. You think that you're reading this chapter of *Mr. Robot and Philosophy*, but perhaps you have been hypnotized into believing that. Best not to think about it too much, and read on, just in case. If Elliot can't rule out the hypnotism scenario, says the philosophical skeptic, then he doesn't really know anything at all.

This is exactly what Descartes was up to in his *Meditations on First Philosophy*. He thought that if you couldn't rule out that you were a mad man, or dreaming, or a victim of a deceiving evil demon, then you couldn't properly be said to have knowledge of any sort. Descartes ultimately believed that by proving God's existence he could rule out the various skeptical scenarios, but unfortunately for Descartes, his arguments for the existence of God failed pretty miserably, and skepticism is a considerably larger part of his philosophical legacy than he would have liked.

The Philosophical Trouble with Elliot

So if Descartes and the philosophical skeptics are right, then no one has any knowledge of the external world as it presently appears, nor do they have knowledge of the past, as once could just as easily be deceived about things in the past. For example, the Evil Demon or a really good hypnotist could make someone believe that certain things happened in the past, when they, in fact, did not. Or, for that matter, you could have dreams about the past, which include events that didn't really happen. This is the predicament, says the skeptic, that everyone finds themselves in. This situation for Elliot is considerably worse.

The reason that things are so much the worse for Elliot is that while the skeptical scenarios we've been discussing apply to everyone, 1. there are countless others—for example, for all you know you're a brain in a vat, or hooked into the Matrix, or some sort of Berkeleyan idealism (from the philosopher George Berkeley) in which there is no physical world is true—and some of these apply to Elliot, even if they don't apply to others, and 2. some of the ones that apply to everyone apply to Elliot even more than they do to others. A closer look at some of Elliot's particular circumstances will reveal precisely why this is the case.

Elliot in the Sky with Diamonds

One of the first things we learn about Elliot is that he is a drug abuser, and not just a recreational drug user—he's a full blown addict who uses a variety of drugs, which he sometimes mixes (although he's hoping to quit, so he measures out his doses). While his main drug is morphine, he also takes ecstasy with his girlfriend Shayla on occasion. Ecstasy, aka MDMA, causes mild hallucinations. On other occasions, he takes suboxone, which may cause hallucinations (some report that it does, some report that it does not). From the fact that Elliot is taking hallucinatory drugs, it's not difficult to construct a skeptical argument.

The skeptical argument from hallucinogens goes something like this:

1. I don't know that I'm not currently on hallucinogens (e.g., ecstasy or suboxone).

2. If I don't know that I'm not currently on hallucinogens, then I don't know that what I'm currently experiencing (seeing, hearing, touching, tasting) or remembering is real.

3. Therefore, I don't know that what I'm currently experiencing or remembering is real.

The first premise for this argument is supported by the fact that if I know that I sometimes do take hallucinatory drugs, then I'm never in a position to rule out that I've taken them recently and part of my hallucination is that I believe that I didn't take them. The second premise stems from the fact that drugs such as ecstasy (and to a lesser extent suboxone) by design alter what a user experiences (that's the whole point of drugs that make you hallucinate). The conclusion, of course, follows logically from the two premises. The payoff is that people who might be hallucinating at any given time are not in the same position as people who are not hallucinating to know what's real. Even if there were some way to overcome the more general skeptical worries that Descartes raises, it doesn't help people like Elliot.

To make matters worse (at least from Elliot's vantage point), he may not be taking drugs. How is this worse, you ask? In the episode "eps1.3_da3m0ns.mp4" Elliot is out of morphine and suboxone, and his supplier, Shayla, is dead. Elliot decides for the good of the mission (you need your wits about you, if you're going to bring the world's largest corporation to its knees), that he should go cold turkey, and he does. During this time Elliot begins to detox and has several extremely vivid hallucinations, including one in which he believes that he is purchasing more heroin. So, in Elliot's case, even when he's not taking drugs, he's at risk of experiencing drug based hallucinations.

Life Is but a Dream . . .

In addition to being a hallucinatory drug user, Elliot, on occasion, has extremely vivid dreams. Descartes rightly pointed out that at any given moment you can't tell whether you're dreaming, but instead having very vivid dream experiences, such that they seem real. Later (in the sixth and final meditation), Descartes suggests that perhaps there is a quality that dreams have that is distinct from reality. While most scholars who work on Descartes's *Meditations* don't find his response to his own dream argument very satisfying, let's grant for the moment that it's fine, and that it's not that difficult to distinguish dream states from regular states. The question is, is this response available to Elliot?

One thing that the writers of the show have built into *Mr. Robot* is that Elliot has extremely vivid realistic dreams (consider his dreams in the pivotal scenes in the penultimate episode of Season Two where, through lucid dreaming, Elliot gets Mr. Robot to reveal facts about Tyrell). In fact, one of the lines that the writers are pushing throughout the series is that the distinction between dream states and waking states is not as clearly distinct as people suppose (recall Whiterose—the leader of the Dark army—asking Angela—Elliot's best friend—"Who is to say that a dream cannot be real?").

So, it's easy to construct a skeptical argument for dreaming just like the one we had for hallucinations, and it will have considerably more force for anyone whose dreams are indistinguishable from reality. Elliot, at any given moment, cannot know whether what he's experiencing is just a dream, even if most of the rest of us can.

What Was It, Again, that Socrates Said?

An even more pressing skeptical argument for Elliot's not being a proper knower stems from the fact that he is quite literally insane. We learn early in the series that he has psychological issues. For example, we learn that he has pretty severe social anxiety disorder. As time goes on we learn that his memory is not reliable. This is most apparent when he tries to kiss Darlene, only to have her ask him whether he remembers that he is her brother. When we're first introduced to Darlene, it appears that Elliot has not met her prior to his being recruited by Mr. Robot for the attack on E Corp. We later come to find out, he's known her nearly his whole life (she's his kid sister by a year or two).

Even more pronounced than his memory issues, is the fact that Elliot has something like dissociative identity disorder, perhaps in combination with schizophrenia, stemming from PTSD. His specific diagnosis is not made explicit on the show, but no matter what the correct diagnosis is, he hallucinates like crazy. He regularly sees, converses, and casually interacts with people who aren't there (for example, Mr. Robot), and he interprets events that are occurring in his life in non-realistic ways.

Two events illustrate this nicely. On one occasion Elliot experiences Mr. Robot pushing him off a pier. This injures him severely. Later it is made clear to the audience that Mr. Robot was not there (he had been dead for several years, at that point) and Elliot hurled himself off the pier. An even better example of Elliot failing to experience reality occurs over the first several episodes of Season Two. Here the audience is led to believe that after the hacking of E Corp Elliot has turned over a new leaf, and is attempting to impose order on his life. He meets with friends at regular times, joins a group to talk about his issues, watches pick-up basketball games at a regular time each day, sets aside some time to write, and so forth. It turns out that Elliot is in prison the whole time, and is never aware of this fact.

These examples provide us with an even stronger reason for drawing the skeptical conclusion that Elliot fails to have knowledge of the things in his world. If at any given moment you're hallucinating for reasons of insanity, then you're never justified in believing anything. Elliot just can simply not be said to be a knower.

Is the situation all that bad? In fact, it's worse. Descartes famously held that even though he might be deceived by an evil demon into believing that the world was not as it appeared, he can always know how things seem to him. That is, he has a kind of special access to his own internal mental states that comes via introspection. One of the more interesting plot twists of *Mr. Robot* has Mr. Robot, who is now just a figment of Elliot's imagination, actually hiding things that Elliot knows from him. Somehow Mr. Robot prevents Elliot from knowing what happened on the night that E Corp was hacked and for several weeks after. It turns out that there are things that some inaccessible part of Elliot knows, but that Elliot himself fails to know. Socrates is best known for admonishing people to "Know thyself." This is precisely what Elliot, as his Mr. Robot persona, prevents himself from doing.

The Knowledge (Un)Problem

Socrates, in Plato's *Meno*, addresses what has come to be called "The Knowledge Problem." The idea is that knowledge is something like justified, true belief, but it's not clear what's so special about having knowledge, if having mere true beliefs gets you the same result.

Elliot, as we've seen, lacks knowledge, because, given his propensity to believe things that aren't true, always lacks justification for his belief. But it's not clear that he's any worse off for not being a knower in many cases. Elliot is still able to bring down E Corp, send the pedophile ring leader to jail, and find out important information about people in his life. At least with respect to these sorts of things it just doesn't matter that Elliot fails to have knowledge. He's still a hero (of sorts).

IV

Politics Is for Puppets

10
If It Isn't Justified Is It Still My Revolution?

JOHN ALTMANN

I know you're reading this chapter right now. Hello, friend.

I wonder, are you even real? Have you come to check in on me? It doesn't matter, I wouldn't believe you regardless of what you answer anyway.

I'm glad you're here. You see I was just returning to a crumbling house with a bare fridge and dimming lights all the while my anxiety makes sleep a product of luxury. But that's fine because the corporations that can easily afford to sleep at night have provided me with the proper tools to numb myself from all that's going on and dying around me. Why worry about my college debts or that I am just one of the many victims of the forty-hour workweek when I can play this game on my phone, beat my high score, and medicate myself for another day all while I stuff the pockets of a filthy rich parasite who sneezes the equivalent of my medical bills everyday of their miserable life?

Can you tell that I'm angry, friend? I'm sorry; I didn't mean to scare you. I have actually had a lot on my mind lately. You see a few months ago, I joined the organization known as fsociety. They were a rag tag group of people like me that were fed up with having our blood sucked by rich scumbags and corporations whose only green cause is the money they print while they do unspeakable damage to the planet.

When I joined fsociety they told me that they were going to start a revolution, by committing the greatest act of hacking imaginable: a hack that would result in the largest scale of wealth redistribution in human history. Can you imagine it, friend? Think about your children while you're reading this. fsociety could send them to any college they want. Think about your bills, they are no longer making you live on the edge of poverty. It's a beautiful revolution isn't it?

To think it's all done right with a simple computer. But then I got to thinking, that's the mistake and arrogance of the world today isn't it? We have destroyed the line between the digital and the physical to the point that we no longer see any difference between the two. With a few keystrokes we can reduce a woman who was having a fun day at the beach to tears because we commented anonymously about how fat she looks in her bathing suit. Or in the case of fsociety, we made James Plouffe, EVP of Technology at E Corp, put a gun in his mouth and commit suicide on national television. We took his life away because he had everything financially invested in Evil Corp and our hack devastated his financial security. Now, you may look at such an event and say that Plouffe was just another bug that got stepped on by the boot of revolution. But I can't help but see him as a husband, father, and grandfather. I can't help but see him as a human being. With a few keystrokes, we took that human being and we murdered him.

Now you might be asking yourself, friend, what kind of rabbit hole you fell in and the answer is in truth just another question. Indeed, you could say it is *the* question that concerns the very act and consequences of the 5/9 hack itself. That question is: can a revolution ever be unjustified? Can a revolution ever commit acts so disgusting they tarnish the very ends they were trying to achieve? Or is a revolution only unjustified when it fails? When it has to answer for all the blood it has shed and lives it has taken with nothing to show for it?

Take my hand, friend. Let's walk this path together. C:/>Moral Philosophy. Don't be scared. Remember you're not even real. So press Enter and let's see if it truly is the case that anything goes and everyone's a target in a state of war and revolution.

The Conservative Condemnation

When I think about fsociety and our 5/9 hack, I think about all the similarities that exist between us and our revolution, and the people who ignited the French Revolution. Much like how we're fighting wealth inequality and the abuses of power that take place in the world by taking down corporations like E Corp, the people of France fought against the inequality and abuses of their age. They overthrew their monarchy and were no longer subservient to the church.

Our revolutions share bloodshed, devastating consequences, and very vocal critics. The biggest critic of the French Revolution was political philosopher Edmund Burke (1723–1792), whom many people regard as the founder of modern-day Conservatism. Such a title is appropriate, given how conservatives believe that progress should happen naturally and not all at once, as happens in a state of revolution. It's because of this fact that Burke rejects the idea of revolution altogether as an unjustified act.

Edmund Burke believed that a society was a kind of organism with a deeply rooted history and longstanding traditions. When members of a given society are faced with a problem, they look to that history and those traditions for a solution. Because of this, Burke believed that the growth of society should be incremental and gradual. Revolution promotes the exact opposite kind of change and when Burke looked at revolutionary France, he saw a vacuum of needless bloodshed, unchained chaos, and absolutely no foundation for a new and healthier society after the revolution was over, since there was no foundation that allowed for people to seize power and use it for their own ends. This is why Burke rejects revolution as an unjustified act because to him it always causes a given society's traditions and history to be destroyed thereby leaving it unstable. This insight is one that is proving in its own ways for fsociety and our 5/9 hack much to my fear.

So, friend, you might be thinking, what fears could someone like Burke, whose ideals are the very ones groups like fsociety actively fight against, instill in me? Well for one thing our hack destroyed the American economy which, as you can imagine, had dire consequences. Financial customers of E Corp could only withdraw fifty dollars a day because E Corp credit cards no longer work, people now have to prepay for services putting a further strain on finances, and garbage is piling up and being burned on sidewalks because private businesses can no longer afford waste management. That's not even mentioning the blackout that occurred throughout the entire city.

Why did all of this happen? It happened because we didn't have a plan. This was made evident by the fact that Mr. Robot got arrested. Then Darlene Alderson took the reins, which resulted in fsociety adopting a plan-as-we-go attitude. Susan Jacobs died when we held her in captivity and left her alone with Darlene, who claims it was an accident, but I have my doubts. That fact that fsociety was guilty of poor planning would seem to validate Burke's rejection of revolution entirely. However, Burke's conservatism would have kept E Corp's power in place and enabled the crimes they were able to commit. That can't be right either, so if the answer can't be found on the right, perhaps we should try going left.

Only Revolution Can Make the Necessary Marx

Are you still holding that book in your hand, friend? Good, I don't want you to be scared by the mention of Karl Marx. I assure you, friend, that our discussion about Marx will be more productive than the conversations you have about him with people who claim to be revolutionary because they bought a Che Guevara shirt on Amazon that was most likely mass produced in a factory with poor conditions, all the while they're sipping on their Starbucks latte. Because Marx wasn't just a critic of capitalism, he was a critic of the very group of people capitalism made powerful—the bourgeoisie. The bourgeoisie, according to Marx, is the class that owns all the power and influence in the form of property, wealth, and productive resources.

Meanwhile, the class that Marx passionately supported—known as the proletariat—was the working class. These are the people who produce the wealth and work the machines that keep entities like E Corp running. To frame it in the context of our present struggle, friend, E Corp is the bourgeoisie as they own seventy percent of the global consumer credit industry and their influence extends to technology, manufacturing, and banking. fsociety and those who support us on the other hand, are the proletariat, the working-class people who have been taken advantage of and abused by E Corp. You're probably wondering how we're going to resolve this struggle, right, friend? Well Marx's solution can be summed up in one word: revolution.

Karl Marx sees the struggle between fsociety and E Corp as just another link in the long chain of history. For Marx, historical change has always come about because of a struggle between the forces of two different classes. For example, in the struggle that was the French Revolution, the monarchy and the church would be regarded as the class with the power. The peasants who fought against them would be regarded as the class which is the victim of abuses by the class with power. In Marx's view, all historical conflicts can be boiled down to class struggle.

Marx believed that the struggle to decide the future of history would be the struggle between the bourgeoisie and the proletariat. In other words, friend, the struggle between fsociety and E Corp is the struggle to determine the course of history. Because of these high stakes, Marx saw revolution as a justified means for the proletariat to use because there is no other way to put an end to the class struggle. Only through these means can we give birth to a prosperous and peaceful society.

I know I mentioned many of the drawbacks of the 5/9 hack, but the hack wasn't without its positives. For one thing, we sparked protests around the world. We tapped into the anger of the people over wealth inequality and the corrupt nature of corporations and nurtured it into a revolution. We created a unified front among all the poor and downtrodden that were victims of E Corp's shady business practices. We brought E Corp themselves to their knees, so much so that they sought out China for a bailout after the US government denied them. We also wiped all banking records, essentially giving everyone a clean slate.

Then when there was Phase Two, which saw us blow up E Corp's physical structure that had the necessary information to restructure the economy in their image through their own unique currency. If they would've achieved this goal then they, as the bourgeoisie, would've had complete control over all of us as the proletariat class. We stopped them and their reach of control and every action fsociety has taken has been for that same end. Yes, even though we drove James Plouffe to suicide in the wake of the 5/9 hack and even though Susan Jacobs died "accidentally," they were still parasites and servants to the same people that oppress us and cause tragedies such as the toxic gas leaks in E Corp's factories in New Jersey that killed several innocent people. Still, no matter how adamantly I want to tell myself that, to convince myself of it as I try to sleep at night, the question that consumes me is always: Was there another way?

Only Light Your Torch If There Is No Recourse

So far, my friend, you've seen two roads. The one road was paved by Edmund Burke, who many regard as the founder of what we know today as conservatism. He believes that revolution is inherently bad and therefore an unjustified course of action because it flings any society rich in history and tradition into chaos. We had no plan for the fallout of the 5/9 hack, and because of that cities have been blacked out, trash has been piling up, there are more people in poverty than out of it, and blood was spilled. We didn't create a new society. What we did create was chaos in a society that was unsuspecting.

On the other hand we have the position of Karl Marx, who saw the evils of capitalism and the bourgeoisie, which we see played out by the actions of Evil Corp. Evil Corp is a corporation with a monopoly on people's lives in the form of technology and financial control. They are a corporation that doesn't care about the lives their business practices ruin or even kill as long as it leads to a bigger bottom line. For Marx, only revolution could wrestle away the control such institutions possess and give it to people like us to create our own society and our own future. Otherwise, the bourgeoisie would keep dominating and nothing would change.

These are two very different views, but which one is correct? Perhaps it depends on the conditions that give rise to the revolution. This is what political philosopher Kai Nielsen argues. Nielsen agrees with Marx on the topic of revolution, but only under the condition that no other actions could have been taken to achieve the same result. This idea is illustrated by the work of Elliot's friend Angela. Angela, who lost her mother in that toxic spill, chooses to join E Corp and change the company's practices internally through non-revolutionary means by climbing the corporate ladder and making the necessary changes to the company's practices. The fact that Angela had this path available to her would likely cause Nielsen to doubt the justification and overall legitimacy of our revolution. He may look at us and point to Angela and say that we should be more like her and find ways to spread our message through non revolutionary means.

The only problem is that Angela ultimately failed in her non-revolutionary approach. The moment she stepped into the board room and tried to openly discuss how E Corp's factories could have higher safety standards and practices, her voice was immediately silenced with icy stares and mocking laughter. Phillip Price, while taking an interest in Angela for some reason, was never completely honest with her about the leaks that killed her mother. In the end, Angela's attempt to change E Corp from within was like trying to move a brick wall with sheer force. If Angela, with her good nature and intelligence, couldn't change the actions of the corporation as it needed to be changed non-revolutionarily, is it even possible to change their actions in that way? I think not, and that's why I believe the way fsociety wages this war against E Corp is the only way.

Hitting Save on the Merits of Marxian Revolution

When all is said and done and the arguments have been made, even with all the chaos our actions have unleashed, I still clench my hands into fists in solidarity with Karl Marx. I believe, of the three political theorists presented, it was Marx who was the most realistic about the instability of capitalism and the tension that exists between entities like E Corp and forces like fsociety. I see Burke as being nothing more than an apologist for the powerful with his view that change should be gradual because society is an organism that can only process so much change at once. Why should we drag our heels while E Corp continues to dominate the globe and crack the whip upon all of our backs? No, I find no worth in a philosophy that serves to protect bourgeoisie interests.

But what of Nielsen and his view that a revolution of the kind that Marx imagined was only permissible if there was no other course of action that could be taken? While I certainly find this view more respectable than Burke's, it isn't without its own flaws. The biggest of which being, how would Nielsen view other means? Does he believe that if some liberal college student started a petition online and got even a million signatures calling for E Corp to change their ways that they would? I know in a democratic society such as ours, there are multiple courses of action that anyone who wants to make change take. But all of these courses of action become meaningless in the seemingly indomitable power of global corporations. The revolution that fsociety started was the only realistic option available.

I know you're not real, friend, and maybe this whole chapter is just a figment in my imagination, but I wanted to leave you with these words.

Power is never an accident and neither is greed. The actions taken in the name of these things is cruel and hurts many innocent people purposely. The powerful always have and always will use force on others to get what they want. So if they use force to take from the innocent, the only way we can give back to the innocent is through force in kind. So I will keep wiping out their bank accounts, I will keep making them feel the poverty and fear they make working class people feel everyday of their miserable lives, and I will keep fighting them with a keyboard whose clacking is endless, all with a clear conscience.

Because in my heart I shall always believe, E Corp is an unnecessary evil taken down necessarily by revolutionary force.

11
The Gods Are Dead and Elliot Has Killed Them

RACHEL ROBISON-GREENE

As the virtual curtain rises on Season 2.0 of *Mr. Robot*, fsociety has successfully carried off the 5/9 hack, deleting all records of the massive debts owed to Evil Corp. Elliot is seemingly staying at his mother's house, fighting his morphine addiction and battling with Mr. Robot for control of their body.

It's clear from the first episode that Elliot is a genius. Like so many other geniuses, he is also deeply psychologically disturbed. His hacking brilliance provides him with the tools that he needs to right the countless wrongs of which only he is aware.

It's also clear that Elliot is not a fully functioning adult. Despite his brilliance, he's developmentally stunted in many ways. He struggles to care for himself and his social skills leave much to be desired. The shortcomings in his emotional development probably have much to do with the premature loss of his father, whose death from cancer was directly attributable to the negligent actions of the international conglomerate that Elliot refers to as "Evil Corp."

Elliot recognizes that global economic structures are remarkably unjust, and he knows that it needs to change. He has the tools and the skills to successfully initiate his revolution, but he doesn't have the strength and emotional fortitude to carry it off without adopting the persona of Mr.

Robot—an alternate personality of Elliot's who takes the form of his dead father. Ironically, Elliot, who revolts against the tyrannical authority of corrupt institutions, seems unable to go forward with his plan without the permission of his father.

In Season 2.0, Elliot initiates a game of chess with Mr. Robot. The winner gets control over Elliot's body for good. Fans of the show wait anxiously to see who wins, after all, as much as we love Elliot, the show simply wouldn't be as fun if he were sane. We don't want the titular character of the series to fade into the recesses of Elliot's troubled mind. They play the game repeatedly and tie the game repeatedly. It looks like both characters are here to stay. But that doesn't mean that their relationship will be smooth. Elliot is becoming increasingly uncomfortable blindly following the commands of Mr. Robot.

The Problem of Evil Corp

One of the main plot revelations in Season 2.0 is that Elliot is not actually staying in his mother's house. He has been protecting himself, and the viewers (his "friends") from reality. He is actually in jail. While there, he makes a desperate attempt to rid himself of Mr. Robot. He buys copious amounts of Adderall from Leon and, sure enough, Mr. Robot goes away. Elliot enjoys the absence of his dominating alter ego, but he starts to feel the physical strain after five days without sleep. While high on Adderall, life, at least subjectively, feels like it's going better for Elliot (though it's obvious to viewers that he is behaving far from normally). He temporarily "finds God," and attends what appears to be AA/NA meetings at the chapel.

In the first episode of Season 2.0 ("eps2.1_k3rnel pan1c.ksd"), he can feel that his Adderoll high will soon wear off. He immediately loses religion. A group of down-and-out people sit in chairs arranged in a circle. An enormous stone Jesus hanging on a cross looms over them. Elliot is usually quiet in these meetings, but this time he decides to speak. The group's leader suggests that God can help Elliot. He responds with one of the best monologues of the series (acted with brilliance by Rami Malek).

> Is that what God does, he helps? Tell me, why didn't God help my innocent friend, who died for no reason, while the guilty roam free? Okay, fine, forget the one-offs. How about the countless wars declared in his name? Okay, fine. Let's skip the random meaningless murder for a second, shall we? How about the racist, sexist, phobia soup we've all been drowning in because of *him*? And I'm not just talking about Jesus. I'm talking about all organized religion. Exclusive groups, created to manage control. A dealer, getting people hooked on the drug of hope. His followers, nothing but addicts who want their hit of bullshit to keep their dopamine of ignorance. Addicts afraid to believe the truth, that there is no order, there's no power, that all religions are just metastasizing mind worms meant to divide us so that it's easier to rule us, by the charlatans that want to run us. All we are to them are paying fanboys of their poorly written sci-fi franchise. If I don't listen to my imaginary friend, why the f*#@ should I listen to yours? People think their worship is some key to happiness. But that's just how he owns you. Even I'm not crazy enough to believe that distortion of reality. So f*#@ God. He's not a good enough scapegoat for me.

Elliot here expresses the fundamentals of an argument that is well known in philosophy as "The Problem of Evil." It's an argument against the existence of the Judeo-Christian God. It doesn't work against any conceivable God, but it is thought to show that a God with a certain set of traits—omniscience, omnipotence, and omni-benevolence—is inconsistent with the existence of unnecessary suffering in the world. "Omniscient" means "all knowing." "Omnipotent" means "all powerful." "Omnibenevolent" means "all good." Traditionally, when this argument is offered, "evil" doesn't mean something like "demonic," but instead means something like "unnecessary suffering." Here's the argument:

P1: If evil exists in the world, then God does not exist.

P2: Evils exists in the world.

C: Therefore, God does not exist.

The reasons that we have to accept the first premise of the argument have to do with the nature of God. If he is omniscient (all knowing), then he knows that unnecessary suffering occurs in the world. If he is omnipotent (all powerful), he can stop the evil from taking place. He must be able to do so; after all, if he is omnipotent, there is nothing that he *can't* do. If he is omnibenevolent (all good), then presumably, he would want to stop the unnecessary suffering from occurring. Good human beings don't desire fellow humans to suffer needlessly, and good human beings, surely, can't hope to approach the moral goodness and love of an omnibenevolent God. *Surely,* then, an all good God wouldn't want unnecessary suffering to take place. So, it looks like the existence of unnecessary suffering in the world is incompatible with the existence of God.

The misgivings and frustrations that Elliot vocalizes about God here are expressed everyday by philosophers and laypersons alike, especially when times get particularly rough. When terrorists crashed planes into major US landmarks in 2001, people were left wondering why a just and loving God had allowed such a thing to happen. When Hurricane Katrina raged over New Orleans, killing thousands of people and displacing still more, many lost their faith. When a shooter walked into an elementary school and killed a large group of first graders and some of their teachers, anger at God gave way for many to total disbelief in him.

The sheer extent of income inequality in the United States creates immeasurable amounts of unnecessary suffering on its own. In a country in which the richest one percent of citizens makes more money than the other ninety-nine percent of the citizens combined, injustices manifest themselves in more substantial ways than simply the size of a person's rainy day fund. The rich can afford expensive medications and cutting edge medical care, while many poor people can't afford even the most basic health care. The rich own houses around the world, while a poor person, working full time might never own a home and may struggle to keep a roof over their head.

What's more, powerful corporations continue to hurt the poor and middle class by fighting against regulations that keep the population safe. When profit is the only motivation, the well-being of the citizenry is abandoned. Elliot saw this first-hand as he watched his father die.

God is omniscient, so he knows the economic structure of the United States. He knows the consequences of the enormous disparity. He is omnipotent, so he could have structured it differently, and he *can still* step in and structure it differently. His intervention could be either direct or indirect. Finally, God is omnibenevolent, so, if he existed, he would care about the well being of *all* of his children, not just the rich ones. It's not hard to see why Elliot is so upset.

Elliot's soliloquy is, of course, about more than organized religion. One of the "Gods" that he references in this speech is his own father. He says, "Mr. Robot has become my God, and like all gods their madness takes you prisoner." As the series progresses, Mr. Robot becomes more controlling and Elliot resents it. Mr. Robot is Elliot without any of Elliot's reservations and moral misgivings. Elliot no longer sees any reason to view Mr. Robot as an authority figure, regardless of whether he manifests in the form of Elliot's father.

"God" in this case is also Evil Corp. As Elliot makes plain in countless voiceovers throughout the season, consumers worship at the shrine of materialism with greater devotion and fervor than they ever demonstrated to any God. The cult of materialism is just another organized religion—and we need to exercise the metastasizing mind worm.

The Fanboys of a Poorly Constructed Value System

Elliot is not alone in his belief that a dramatic revision to the basic structure of society is required. To really bring about the change that he wants involves shaking off the mantle of paternalism. It involves saying "No" to the systems and institutions we've been told that we must revere. To really change that structure in a permanent would require not simply an event like a hack, but strength in numbers to avoid the slide of power back to the corrupt elite.

In *On the Genealogy of Morals,* Friedrich Nietzsche describes a power shift of similar magnitude. This shift involved not only a change in power dynamics, but also an inversion of our very system of values themselves. His discussion of this topic describes how such a shift in power might be possible, but it also highlights the conditions under which it could potentially successful. His discussion will have implications for Elliot's revolution.

Nietzsche argues that terms like "good" and "bad" were once life-affirming terms. The noble class reflected on their own traits such as strength, power, intelligence, beauty, wealth, and so on. These seem to be natural human strengths. The term "good" was coined to describe these strengths. The noble class then adopts what Nietzsche calls a, "pathos of distance." From this perspective, they reject the traits that are opposed to the ones that they affirm upon introspection. They reject traits like poverty, impotence, and stupidity. The term "bad" is used to describe these traits.

Of course, not everyone is lucky enough to possess the "good" traits that the master class finds upon introspection. In fact, many possess the traits that are considered "bad." These people are a group that Nietzsche calls the "slave class." In this class, over time, a strong resentment develops. Then, a remarkable thing happens. From the sheer strength of their resentment, the slave class is able to invert the traditional values. The traits that were previously considered "bad" by the master class are given new names and are considered "good."

So, for example, an inability to pursue the goals set by ambition is recast as "humility." An inability to exact revenge is cast as "forgiveness," and so on. It is at this point, also, that the term "evil" is born. The terms that were previously considered "good" by the master class are given new names and are called "evil." Confidence in your own beauty is considered "vanity." Confidence in your skills and intellectual abilities is understood as "arrogance," and so on. These traits are not simply *bad* according to slave morality, they're downright *sinful*.

The resentment of the slave class is powerful enough to invert our system of values. But the new value system is unnatural. Gods are created to reinforce it. The invention of sin and the fear of retribution are powerful enough to keep the desired result of the revolution in place. At the time that Nietzsche was writing, he thought that the value system of the slaves remained in place, that we were still suffering the effects of self-hatred that a rejection of natural human strengths necessarily generates.

Elliot is trying to enact a revolution of similar magnitude. A proportionally very small number of people have become very powerful—powerful enough that they basically run the world. The resentful class is the oppressed class—they are crushed under the weight of the financial power of a small set of billionaires and multinational corporations. Elliot wants to give power back to the people. The people want this too, or at least, it would seem that they do. The 5/9 hack may just be the event that can make that happen.

Unfortunately, there's a significant difference between the case that Nietzsche describes and the one in which Elliot is involved. Unlike the slave class Nietzsche describes, the oppressed people that Elliot hopes to save are complicit in their own subordination. They get something out of it. Through the businesses that they run, the powerful make the daily lives of the people more convenient. The citizenry is enslaved by their own debt, but they would like it less if they weren't.

The world that Elliot finds himself in (and, indeed, the world in which *we* find *ourselves*) is one that is populated by people who scream for change but don't really want to take the steps necessary to bring it about. If we want the world to be run by alternatives to the elite, by alternatives to billionaires with corporate interests, we need to have some value system to which we can commit ourselves that is bigger and more powerful than the system handed to us by the corporate gods. We don't have that, and that is, at least in part, why Elliot's revolution didn't have the effect that he and his cohorts intended. We can't rid ourselves of the dominant system without a new system ready to hand with which to replace it.

God Is Dead

In a passage from *The Gay Science* commonly referred to as "The Parable of the Madman," Nietzsche describes a man, carrying a lantern, who descends into a town shouting, "Where is God? Where is God?" The local atheists that he encounters tease him, and he replies, "Whither is God? I will tell you— we have killed him you and I. All of us are his murderers . . . God is dead. God remains dead. And we have killed him."

The atheists that the madman encounters don't believe that God is literally dead. After all, they believe that he never existed in the first place. Be that as it may, the madman's message is tailored to this exact audience. Or, perhaps, it's tailored to some future version of this type of audience. The madman says:

> I have come too early. My time is not yet. This tremendous event is still on its way, still wandering. It has not yet reached the ears of men. Lightning and thunder require time; the light of the stars requires time; deeds, though done, still require time to be seen and heard. This deed is still more distant from them than some distant stars—*and yet they have done it to themselves.*

Though the madman's audience has given up their belief in God, they are not yet ready to take on the challenge that rejection requires. For Nietzsche, the next evolution of human beings—the Übermensch—will know that the proper way to move on from the death of God is to become Gods themselves. They must become creators.

Elliot, is presented to us as a socially awkward, emotionally stunted, drug-addicted member of the counter-culture. He certainly isn't what we would likely picture when we think of the next step in the evolution of human beings. That certainly seems like a perfectly reasonable conclusion to draw. At first. Until what we have been suspecting all along is confirmed—Elliot *is* Mr. Robot, or, to be more precise, Elliot sometimes manifests as Mr. Robot, who is purely a product of Elliot's mind. This means that every time Mr. Robot handled a situation like a stone cold badass, it was really *Elliot the badass*. Elliot the Übermensch.

When we think of the totality of Elliot's actions, the sum total of the behaviors of all of his personas—a character emerges who is bent on bringing about a new world of his own creation. He is done accepting the power dynamics of a world run by ruthless omnipotent corporations. He is done being spoon-fed a value system that dictates luxury without limit for the rich while the poor suffer and die while paying the powerful for the privilege. *fsociety*. Elliot's creating a new one.

12
Why Angela Drops the Whistle

TIM JONES

Thirty-seven minutes into the ninth episode of Season Two ("eps2.7_init_5.fve"), you might think that Angela Moss is just moments away from becoming a national idol.

She's finally about to fulfill the goal that she set up by taking the job with E Corp in the Season 1.0 finale and getting moved to the Risk Management division. She's hacked into files that could expose the role of a gas leak at E Corp's Washington Township plant in the deaths of twenty-six E Corp employees, including her own mom (and Elliot and Darlene's dad.) She's taken this information to the United States Nuclear Regulation Commission and the guy who's looked over it has confirmed it proves an ongoing "substantial and specific danger to public health and safety." Deputy Director Phelps has just met Angela for herself and lauded her actions as heroic.

But then the anonymity that Angela's been promised is threatened by the Deputy Director wanting contact details and confirmation that she works at E Corp. Almost like a switch has gone off in her head, Angela hurries away from the encounter as fast as her designer heels will carry her. She doesn't have a chance to reconsider her decision before being seduced by Whiterose into severing contact with the lawyer who's been working with the families affected by the gas leak. It's looking like Angela won't be paying another visit to the Commission at any point in the near future.

What Angela so very nearly becomes is a *whistleblower*, or an individual who informs on another individual, or an organization or company, which is engaged in illegal or immoral activities. The term is usually applied to an individual reporting behavior in his or her *own* workplace to a body outside that workplace, just like Angela is in the process of doing. *The Wall Street Journal* tells us that it originated in the early twentieth century, depicting informing as a similar action to a sports referee blowing a whistle to call-out a foul and award a penalty.

While the connotations of the word were initially little better than those of "rat" or "snitch," consumer rights advocate Ralph Nader sought in the 1970s to rehabilitate it as a term that could portray informing as an act of heroic struggle against corruption embedded within corporate and government practice, which would remain invisible and continue to harm the public unless people in the know were encouraged to speak out. Deputy Director Phelps would totally agree with him. She goes as far as telling Angela that the Commission is reliant on people like her if it's to protect the American public from corporate malpractice.

So why does Angela back off so fast? It's not just strange because her whistleblowing puts her on the cusp of a revenge she's wanted for decades. Surely as soon as she's known as the woman behind the whistle, she'd receive glowing praise from every citizen who hears her name, for helping make the country a better place, where the little people are less likely to become faceless collateral damage to the money-making schemes of companies like E Corp. The President himself would want to know all about this woman from New Jersey, so she can be decorated with the highest honors for her selfless defence of the nation's safety. Right?

Maybe not. If we look at responses to actual cases of what might obviously seem an ethically unimpeachable act, then Angela's sudden about-turn on hearing that her name and status as E Corp employee will both be associated with the leak becomes entirely understandable. Despite Nader's attempts at reframing how we all see whistleblowing, whistleblowers aren't always treated very nicely. They're mistreated not only by the organizations against which they speak out, but by the members of the public too who you'd think would see how much their country would benefit from the whistleblower's bravery.

Courts of Law

The treatment faced by at least one whistleblower who lost her anonymity shows us why Angela was so worried.

You and Angela will both have heard about the high-profile case of whistleblower and former US Army intelligence analyst Chelsea Manning, who released highly sensitive material to the online database WikiLeaks. The material, which WikiLeaks quickly made available to the world, included video documentation of US airstrikes in Iraq and Afghanistan, along with hundreds of thousands of military reports and diplomatic cables. This information revealed US complicity in civilian casualties and failure to investigate allegations of torture and child abuse, amongst many other sensitive matters, including military actions in Yemen that the government denies to this day.

Manning was charged with a number of offences, including aiding the enemy (which could've led to a death sentence, had this not been dropped), espionage, and theft. She was sentenced in August 2013 to thirty-five years at the Leavenworth Disciplinary Barracks, where she remained until her sentence was pretty unexpectedly commuted in one of the final acts of Obama's presidency.

Manning's case highlights the *legal* risks of whistleblowing. Perhaps Angela had a sudden image of spending the rest of her life in solitary in a high-security prison, especially since the incriminating evidence she's giving to the Commission was obtained through illegal hacking of another employee's computer.

She might've been reassured by the distinction that she was considering whistleblowing against a private company, rather than against an organ of federal government. This difference alone would grant her a much greater defense against the imprisonment faced by Manning. Manning's actions would only have been covered by the limited protection offered by the Military Whistleblowers Protection Act of 1988, which guarantees this sort of whistleblower safety if they pass their information on only to Congress, an Inspector General, or any third party who has been officially designated as appropriate for receiving said information. So as long as you leak your evidence of state-sponsored law breaking to one of a small pool of people that the state says you're allowed to leak it to, you're basically fine. The entire internet doesn't really count.

As a private whistleblower, Angela would be significantly less likely to end up behind bars, thanks to statutory protections adopted by the New York State legislature and Federal Government. Even obtaining information about illegal actions through illegal means can potentially get a free pass. These protections would prevent Angela from facing retaliatory action from E Corp itself too, meaning that she could even have kept her exact position in the company if she'd wanted to continue encouraging change from the inside like former employee Terry Colby suggests she do, however much this might've made her next day at work pretty awkward.

A look at workplacefairness.org suggests that her whistleblowing would be covered by these protections from at least two angles: in terms of E Corp having breached its health and safety responsibilities towards its own employees (like Eliot's dad) *and* in terms of E Corp engaging in activities that present a 'substantial and specific danger to public health and safety.' Radiation getting into the water just isn't good for anyone.

So Ralph Nader must've been at least partially successful in persuading federal and state government that whistleblowing has a valuable role to play in preserving ethical and moral values in the face of private companies that seek to breach these values for their own profit margins. The government itself recognizes that the best society comes about when the law leaves citizens feeling secure enough to follow their own ethical imperatives over the interests of their employers, when the latter are clearly in breach of the greater good. Just so long as it's not the government itself who's doing the breaching . . .

Courts of Public Opinion

So does this level of protection mean that Angela's sudden panic was unnecessary? Does it mean that had she known all about the security that the law would offer her, she'd have given her details to Deputy Director Phelps without a moment's hesitation? Perhaps not, if you consider that Chelsea Manning's case shows that legal action is only *one* part of the punishment whistleblowers can face for acting with the very best of intentions.

Manning's actions have been torn apart by public opinion as much as by the law. If you buy that her leaks put American staff and civilians across the world in greater danger, then they could be the ultimate betrayal of the same countrymen who—as a member of the armed services—she'd vowed to protect. But her support website at chelseamanning.org includes the following quote from US founding father Patrick Henry: "The liberties of a people never were, nor ever will be, secure, when the transactions of their leaders will be concealed from them." Maybe, then, it was the government itself that was the betrayer, in this case, of the very principles upon which the United States was founded, while Manning has sacrificed years of her life to restore the ideals our ancestors fought and died for. What do you think?

While I'm guessing that Angela would see the value of Manning's actions over the condemnation of her accusers, her sudden fear at Deputy Director Phelps prying into her personal details might be motivated by her internet browsing having led her to a 2013 poll by Rasmussen Reports, which shows the majority of the public siding against the former intelligence analyst. Fifty-two percent of Americans regard Manning as a traitor to her country, while only seventeen percent consider her a hero.

If you're in Manning's situation, you might think an outpouring of public support will help make any punishment from the authorities more tolerable. Instead you could end up getting flamed from all sides. Knowing that a majority of the people you were trying to empower don't think any more highly of you than the authorities is likely to make every moment of confinement that bit harder to bear. Obama might eventually have thought positively enough of her actions to have her sentence commuted, but given that he's being flamed for his decision by people who still see Manning as an enemy collaborator, it's no guarantee that the general public are going to feel any kinder towards her.

Whistleblower Blues

So Angela probably has extra legal protection on her side even despite her *il*legal hacking. She's also got the fact that her whistleblowing would've honored the memories of the US civilians already killed by E Corp's actions and made it less likely for the Washington Township plant to create any future victims, rather than putting additional US civilians in danger, like our government argued Manning was doing. Yet it's still very possible that the court of public opinion would've shown Angela the same condemnation and made her life hell.

Research into whistleblowing in the US, Canada, and United Kingdom shows that life for a whistleblower can be pretty grim. Even if Angela escaped being arrested or fired and wanted to continue working to make E Corp a better company from the inside, she'd be vulnerable to being ostracized by her fellow employees, both those above her and the colleagues on the same rung of the ladder.

You might think this an odd reaction. We've already looked at the moral and ethical worth of whistleblowing as a tool that can force society to hold itself to the highest standards. Surely no one who actually works at E Corp would *want* to be employed by a company which is okay with poisoning people's health, right? They'd surely be grateful to Angela for speaking out and making their workplace a morally purer environment—one they can enter holding their head up high as they step off the subway and walk through the turnstile each morning, rather than one that's going to taint them with scandal by association.

Well, these noble sentiments might not come all that cheap, if the secrets spilled by the whistleblower cause such disruption that the business is threatened with closure. Look at the former energy giant Enron, which filed for bankruptcy in 2001 after whistleblowers revealed a business model based on massive accountancy fraud. Enron's collapse cost thousands of jobs and billions of dollars in pension plans. Employees who'd transferred their assets into Enron shares were ruined. Imagine being an E Corp employee who ends up without your regular source of income and gets your pension taken away, just because the lady who started a few months ago wants to be a hero.

And I reckon there's deeper, more primal motivations that make appreciating the moral worth of Angela's actions pretty difficult, beyond the financial. Since the dawn of humanity, we've survived everything the world threw at us by gathering together in tribes. We can do so much in the face of seemingly insurmountable odds when we pull together and combine our resources. When food becomes scarce and when rivals come threatening your territory, you need to know that everyone in your tribe is sticking together and working as a single harmonious entity.

If any one member is thinking of going off to another group of people and dropping your tribe's important secrets, this could be the difference between life and death. It could give another tribe the advantage that means that it survives in the struggle for existence, over your own people. And so I reckon that scepticism towards an individual who refuses to be a team player became so ingrained into our psyches tens of thousands of years ago that we're just as willing to demonize someone who speaks out against a body of people we're a member of today as we were back then. What's the group of people we work alongside for five out of every seven days (assuming E Corp respects weekends) if not a modern-day equivalent of a tribe? I think the similarities make it very easy for our subconscious minds to see it this way.

So no matter how morally worthwhile Angela's whistle-blowing would be, she's fighting against the tribal survival instincts that ensured our species got off the ground. And there's another, more selfish reason too that would account for the criticism she'd get from her fellow employees. Imagine if you were working at E Corp for years before Angela rocked up from nowhere. You might have seen the news reports about the Washington Township leak and E Corp's complicity in a number of deaths and just hoped the rumours would go away. You might have hated yourself a little for doing this, but hey, you needed the job. And not everyone is brave enough to put their head above the firewall and face down their bosses—why should you be judged for showing the same caution that millions of other Americans would too?

But then someone comes along who isn't prepared to let the rumors fade away and who's brave enough to do what it takes to make absolutely sure they don't. So how do you feel now? Making out that it's completely okay to ignore the bad stuff you suspect your workplace is getting up to is so much easier when everyone else is doing the same. When someone shows that it's possible to speak out, you might well feel a massive sense of cowardice for not having done the same. The morality of the whistleblower only highlights the immorality of all the workers who sat in silence. And so if these other workers are to keep their sense of worth, the whistleblower needs to be demonized. If his or her actions are depicted as self-serving, or money-grabbing, or mentally unstable, then his or her colleagues can continue to make out that they're the ones in the right.

Angela's Choice

Let's say Angela handed over both the evidence against E Corp and her contact details and then returned to work the next day. Let's say she escaped any legal ramifications, because the results of her illegal hacking were proven to be in the public interest. And let's say that when E Corp tried to fire her, she argued successfully that this was vindictive retaliation for actions in the public interest and so they were forced to keep her on. She's in the clear, right?

The Nuclear Regulation Commission would see E Corp put before the courts and every day its employees would worry about the company being closed down. They'd look at the woman who started all this and whisper to each other behind her back about how an act they'd very readily begin to depict as Angela's own self-aggrandizing moral crusade has put every one of their livelihoods at risk. They'd shun her across the desk and at the water-cooler. She'd stop getting asked to any gatherings over lunch or at the swanky bars her co-workers visit after work.

Every day she'd feel more and more shunned, more and more isolated. Her daily life at E Corp might even get so hard that she forgets the worthy goal that led her to take the job and she hands in her resignation. Who's then going to employ the woman who's known across the US for leading her previous employer to end up in court? Her isolation at the hands of E Corp's other employees could still lead to long-term unemployment, even if the management is legally bound to leave her alone.

And I reckon that the same psychological reasons for her own co-workers to hate her would mean that a decent proportion of the wider public would do too. Rather than a hero who's standing up for public safety, everyone would see Angela as the potential person in their own company who'd put *their* jobs and reputations at risk, the reminder of potential betrayal lurking within the ranks of their own tribe. And if they bump into her out and about in Manhattan, they'd treat her accordingly.

Cliff Baxter, an Enron executive who'd agreed to testify about the company's financial practices before Congress, was found shot dead in his car on the morning of January 25th 2002. His suicide note to his family said "Where there was once great pride now it's gone."

Whistleblowing can lead to a lonely, bullied existence. It might be an ethically sound course of action, conducive to the greater good and a better, safer society. Yet it's an act that our tribal roots and our need for financial security mean many of us will find it very difficult to support. Perhaps this is E Corp's greatest security, beyond any it can buy itself from the most expensive New York law firms. That if Angela had gone ahead with her whistle-blowing and become publically associated with their downfall, the people might condemn her, rather than hail her as someone who's made their lives that bit safer. That'd be enough to make anyone back away.

V

Power Belongs to the People Who Take It

13
How to Become a Revolutionary

ROB LUZECKY AND CHARLENE ELSBY

Mr. Robot is a revolutionary figure. Though he's a hallucination, he both recruits and unifies a disparate group of individuals that go on to perpetrate a hack which undermines the capitalist structure of the Western world.

This sort of revolutionary event seems to be unaccounted for in all of traditional political philosophy. For many centuries philosophers have analyzed the nature of the State, the nature of the citizen, and the nature of rights, but these discussions seem to be wholly inadequate to define the revolutionary group, whose leader at one point describes himself as an analog of a computer virus that plugs itself into various networks only to scramble their codes.

Maybe we can get some insight into this strange new kind of revolution by looking at the work of Gilles Deleuze and Félix Guattari. Deleuze was a philosopher, Guattari a psychiatrist and political revolutionary. These two writers joined forces after the revolutionary events of May 1968 in France, a revolution that was nipped in the bud, partly because all the supposed professional revolutionaries such as the Communist Party, came together to support the government

Deleuze and Guattari conceive of capitalism as a system governed by "flows," especially flows of investment capital and flows of labor. The flows are "coded," or limited by social expectations. Flows can be interrupted, for instance by hackers, and so hackers can become revolutionaries if they interrupt various flows and threaten the survival of the system.

The hackers embody the concept of the "war-machine." While most of us go through our days happily completing our appointed tasks, driving the speed limit, and paying our taxes, the war-machine is that odd type of entity that is defined by its capacity for radical betrayal of the social contract. Altogether different from mere rule-breakers and certainly from law-abiding citizens, the war-machine is a mercurial grouping that floats at the margins of any social configuration, like a bunch of disgruntled corporate drones who refuse to take off their hoodies, insist on consuming drugs, and destroy lives just as happily as they forge fragile unities.

What's remarkable and perhaps most vexing about Mr. Robot's revolution is that by the end of Season One, Evil Corp is seemingly brought to its nadir without a gun being fired. We suggest that this type of revolution conforms to the model set forth by Deleuze and Guattari. Instead of bringing destruction, Mr. Robot heralds a fascinating revolution where the very concept of limitation (more than any particular corporation or governmental institution) is an enemy to be attacked. According to Deleuze and Guattari, we become revolutionaries at the very moment we turn up our hoods, turn on the lights in the abandoned arcade, and set about trying to bring something new to the world. The moment we act in defiance to those who tell us we cannot is the moment we become revolutionary, and this revolution, at least in Deleuze's, Guattari's, and Mr. Robot's eyes, is guaranteed success precisely because it is an affirmation of our capacity to act in a world populated by states and corporations that try to condition our actions at every turn.

Everything Is Coded, Everything Flows, and Mr. Robot Becomes Something Else

It isn't surprising that flows give rise to the hacker collective Mr. Robot, since the "big bad" that is the object of their revolutionary attack is the economic entity know as Evil Corp. Deleuze and Guattari identify their concept of flows in relation to a discussion of the movement of capital, goods, and data in the global economic system.

You wake-up and you stumble out of bed on your way to a job as a coder, cyber security analyst, computer repairer (IT guy or gal), or neighborhood pot dealer, and you are a participant in flows of transfer that pass along the surface of the Earth. You activate your smart-phone and click your least favorite but most over-used social-media app and read a series of headlines about recent events in some country—perhaps a whole bunch of ill-informed, mostly uninterested citizens just elected a leader who (to all appearances) is a racist, misogynist xenophobe, and the whole country is going through some serious voters' remorse.

As you're transfixed by the scroll of the stories, you forget for a moment (or two, or three) that your awareness of these events is only the consequence of an immense number of economic and social processes. Deleuze and Guattari consider these processes to be "flows." They further define the concept of flows as the correlate of their concept of codes.

Anthropologists, economists, and even a few philosophers have noticed that back in the day, some day before you and I existed, societies tended to operate through reference to a series of codes. There were familial codes that told you whom you could marry, and for whom you had to milk the cow, and with whom you could share the milk. There were religious codes that told you what god you were to worship, which buildings you could worship in, and the particular orientation in which to place yourself relative to the sacrificial (but now mostly symbolic) altar. There were even legal codes that told you whom you could kill and what constituted legal authority. The important point about all these codes is that they didn't encourage too much.

Borrowing from Nietzsche's concept of the "moralist" (for instance, the person who shouts "No" in the attempt to stop you from pushing yourself off of boardwalk at Coney Island), Deleuze and Guattari see codes as the very peculiar class of concepts that contains all the things you are told that you can't do. With reference to so-called "primitive" societies

141

(which really just means "societies that are historically prior, and in which the members are not so hoity-toity as to constantly and obsessively demand to have the latest fancy thing"), Deleuze and Guattari use the phrase "rigid segmentary code" to denote particularly pernicious religious, familial, and legal codes that set about parsing human life through reference to a series of conditions that allow for the emergence of a series of instructions about how we should not be in their world (Deleuze and Guattari, *A Thousand Plateaus*, pp. 210–13).

Flows are subject to codification. We see this explicitly with the emergence of money—defined as the paper and shiny stuff of value that people who are more important than you collect from you—and the tax code—defined as that byzantine aggregation of stipulations that allows Evil Corp's executives to give up virtually none of their money to the government. On our best and most charitable of days, we might think that the money we pay in taxes goes toward making our lives better, and in some very narrow cases this is true—in places like Canada and the UK, some of your tax dollars go toward funding a universal healthcare system—but Deleuze and Guattari argue that the process of taxation is, in effect, the State taking money out of the capitalist system so that it (the State) can insert itself into the lives of citizens.

Money, say Deleuze and Guattari, "is fundamentally inseparable, not from commerce, but from taxes as the maintenance of the apparatus of the State" (*Anti-Oedipus*, p. 197). We pay our money to a government, and this takes it out of the flow of capital. The story Deleuze and Guattari are telling us is one where the government takes some of our money, with the single aim of advancing the State's most basic goal of gaining recognition as an authority in our lives.

Were we to imagine a situation in which money was not subject to taxation, we might picture something like videogame arcade, or even the arcade of the market place, where we gave up our money to get something we desired— the joy that we get from shooting asteroids to the music of *Jaws*, or the joy we get from the shiny trinket from far-off lands, it doesn't matter. In this situation, money is simply and wonderfully connecting us to that fantasy we live in a pixelated universe or connecting us to the far distant lands that produced the trinket. The only thing limiting the flow of the money in this case is our capacity to imagine, and, in a very real sense, this is no limit at all. Taxation, however, imposes an artificial limit on this money, it directs it to the very specific and utterly singular end of the maintaining the State.

Now you might think all of this is not so bad; perhaps the government does a great job of telling you what you want and using its authority for good ends. Deleuze and Guattari suggest this when they refer to the "absolute limit" of "the wilderness, where decoded flows run free, as the end of the world, the apocalypse" (p. 176). Our spending habits are regulated, our taxes paid, and the government inserts itself a bit into our lives, shaping our desires, which, if left to run amok, would amount to the end of the world and all that's in it.

Yet the real price we pay in avoiding the catastrophe of unregulated desires is the threat of over-regulation. In coding our desires through both demanding taxes and setting itself up as the authority that provides lovely social programs and electrical grids, the government enacts a system of "infinite debt," where we the citizens and the hackers, the philosophers and the students are trapped in a web of coded desires where we feel that our very existence is divested from us as we complacently, perhaps even smilingly ride the subway on the way home from an exhausting day of following all the rules.

Elliot Alderson is also on that subway. He's the guy in the hoodie hunched over against the rail. He's been working and failing long enough, and he's tired of having his existence coded. He's tired of feeling like he is not living up to some artificial standard of what a person should be. His plan is to erase all the debt records, and thereby erase debt, which would have the effect of setting him free. This plan was hatched and gets enacted in a world where Deleuze and Guattari's diagnoses of the function debt and code apply. When he hallucinates on the subway, when he breaks from reality, Elliot is becoming something fundamentally opposed to any attempts to control desire. He's becoming something essentially dangerous to any array of institutional forces which try to quell him. He's becoming a revolutionary force. He's becoming what Deleuze and Guattari call a "nomadic war-machine."

Becoming a Nomadic War-Machine

When most people hear the phrase "war-machine," perhaps they think of something big, menacing, and heavily armored, like the Sherman tanks that were instrumental in winning the land battles in Europe during World War II. Or perhaps they think of a certain comic-book character who's quite a bit more agile than anything that chewed up the landscape during the first great battle against fascists.

When people think about nomads, they probably think of that band of warriors on horseback who rode across the plains of Asia, laying waste to everything, until they ran out of land at the southern shores of South Korea. Deleuze has something a bit different in mind when he uses these terms. Deleuze uses the phrase "a nomadic distribution" (Deleuze, *Difference and Repetition*, pp. 36–37) to describe a way of thinking about physical space and your relation to the stuff in that space. This might seem like a sort of benign way to begin thinking like a revolutionary, but it is not. The way we think about space and boundaries will change the value of everything, and it does define the nature of Mr. Robot's revolution.

For the nomadic war-machine, space is infinite, because it's non-segmented. In a nomadic distribution, space is fundamentally open (*A Thousand Plateaus*, pp. 379–384). The nomad sees the world like a subway train where all the doors between the individual cars and all the poles and armrests separating the seats are simply not there. This concept of there being no boundaries in space implies that there are no boundaries between things in space. When we conceive of our lived world as something that is without internal division we're thinking of the world as the sort of place where measurements do not apply.

This amounts to the claim that there is, in fact, no measure in the world. In a world of nomadic distribution, there's simply no way to distinguish between what's bigger and what's smaller, what's longer and what's shorter. For Deleuze and Guattari, this lack of measurement applies to spatial things (like corporate headquarters, data vaults, and server rooms) and also to the capacities of a rag-tag group of hackers.

If we don't know how big or small something is, and if we have no way of figuring out where the thing is located, then we cannot determine what it can or cannot do. When a thing cannot be localized in space, its capacities to change the world cannot be determined. The lack of limit in a spatial sense implies an ambiguity of a thing's powers. Measure is one of the means we use to carve up things into different types (in a metaphysical sense). In taking away the concept of measure, Deleuze takes away the concept of measuring differences in powers among things. When we apply the nomadic concept of space to our rag-tag group of hackers, we discover that they are powerful beyond measure, which is just another way of saying that their powers to change the world are without limit.

But it takes more than a bit of French metaphysics from the late 1960s to change the world. Revolutionaries need to know who and what to ignore. Those engaged in a revolution are constantly told that their cause is futile or misguided. The enemies—those pusillanimous souls like Tyrell Wellick and Phillip Price, who deliberately lie to us, obscure the truth, and settle lawsuits while they set about destroying America from the boardroom of a New York City skyscraper—always tell us that there's nothing to be concerned about, and that our rage is hyperbolic. The revolutionary's most insidious enemy is the person who wears the expensive suit and tells you that you should be complacent and accept the status quo. This is precisely the message that Elliot rejects when he explains to his psychologist that the world is, in fact, a place where all of our choices are already conditioned by those who wish us to be nothing more than pawns ("eps1.1_ones-and-zer0es.mpeg").

Elliot recognizes that most of the choices we face in contemporary culture (the choices between Coke and Pepsi, between Blue Cross and Blue Shield, between McDonalds and Burger King) are designed to give us the illusion of control, when in fact they are merely evidence that we're being controlled. This control is far worse than the control enforced by rubber-bullets and truncheons, in the sense that it aims at precluding the possibility of a revolutionary thought ever occurring. We become docile citizens when our choices are determined. Elliot recognizes that our choices are determined by those who create the options from which we get to choose. By the end of the episode, Elliot recognizes: 1. that these "pre-paid choices" are just different expressions of the choice to be a slave to those—mainly corporate, but sometimes governmental—forces that tell you that there is nothing to be concerned about, and; 2. there is at least one other option—choosing to change the world by constantly resisting any efforts to tell you how you must think (Deleuze and Guattari, *A Thousand Plateaus*, p. 386).

Mr. Robot's Affirmative Revolution

Elliot walks into the arcade with Tyrell, and the lights flicker on. The room is deserted. The hack has been executed, and the revolution has started. All of Evil Corp's financial records have been encoded, and their back-ups have been destroyed. Popcorn starts popping ("eps1.8_m1rr0r1ng.qt").

According to the news, seventeen foreign governments are in "large scale crises, with some on the verge of collapse" ("eps1.9_zer0-day.avi"). In foreign capitals, people have taken to the streets. Closer to home, the president has convened numerous cabinet meetings that have produced no solution. Nobody's credit cards work any more. Darlene's code was executed, and apparently billions of dollars of digital wealth has disappeared from the world markets. People in expensive clothing are running around in office towers. Despite the financial losses, the panic of governments, and protests, nothing substantive seems to have really changed. The lights still come on. Angela still goes to work and gets yelled at by her boss. Elliot too shows up to work and observes that it is not exactly what he thought a revolution would look like ("eps1.9_zer0-day.avi").

On the day before the revolution, we revolutionaries had such very high hopes about what our actions would produce. On the day after the revolution, everything is basically the same. We still have hallucinations of thousands of protestors in Times Square, but we now recognize that they are merely hallucinations. This causes us to question whether our great social movement was really so great. Maybe we revolutionaries are really nothing but a band of outsiders in an abandoned arcade, who are forever out of place, out of step, and cut-off from society.

Sure we attempted to f-society, but on the day after the revolution, maybe we begin to figure out that society doesn't really care. Sure, we can have a party where there's free beer, and sure, Darlene can shout out to the room of oblivious strangers that "We are finally awake" and then, in more hushed tones, "We are finally alive" ("eps1.9_zer0-day.avi"). But none of it really seems to be that big of a deal. We were awake and alive yesterday, and the day before that. If these are the only results of our revolution, then this shows our revolution to be quite sad.

For Deleuze and Guattari (and Mr. Robot) a revolution is really much more personal, and much less sad. For them, the true revolution is accepting yourself as changeable, sometimes very fucked up, sometimes hallucinating, sometimes blacking-out, and sometimes extremely nervous, sometimes extremely stoned being. There's nothing wrong with these. Our real consistency is the fact that we are countless desires, countless drives, and countless aspirations. This consistency is shattered by all the forces of the world that try to tell us that our behavior must fall into a range of acceptability.

The real revolution is an affirmation of all the differences within ourselves, and a recognition that we need not accept

147

any authority that attempts to make us fit into any narrow range of behaviors. Instead of conforming, and hating ourselves for conforming—because we know that all conforming is really just suppressing the infinitude of what we are—we should simply embrace our differences. The real revolution is embracing the chaos of ourselves. The real revolution is simply getting on the subway, getting off at the stop we want, sitting down somewhere and accepting ourselves, by enjoying all the beauty that our difference creates.

14
Is E Corp an Evil Person?

MIA WOOD

Together we can change the world, with E Corp.

—E Corp

Elliot worries, and rightfully so, that some of his perceptions can't be trusted. People he thinks exist, don't, at least not in the way we ordinarily believe they do. Yet Elliot has no doubts about Evil Corp. This is, after all, the multi-national conglomerate allegedly responsible for the death of Elliot and Darlene's father and Angela Moss's mother.

Elliot and Angela are convinced that, in 1993, E Corp's factories in Washington Township, New Jersey, leaked dangerous chemicals. Within two years, twenty-six employees—including Elliot and Darlene's father, Edward Alderson, and Angela's mother—died from leukemia. Surviving family members filed a class action lawsuit, but E Corp argued there was no evidence linking the events at the factories with the diagnoses. The lawsuit was dismissed.

Subsequently, E Corp's holdings both increased and diversified. The conglomerate manufactures computers, phones, and tablets in various parts of the world. It owns E Bank, which operates both a mortgage and consumer credit division—according to fsociety, Evil Corp controls seventy percent of the global consumer credit industry.

E Corp's employee roster has also grown, from sixteen to twenty-seven million, worldwide. At the helm is CEO, Phillip Price. He is more than a figurehead, since at any given time, he pulls any number of strings behind the scenes. After the May 2015 fsociety hack of Evil Corp's digital records and physical back-ups, Price maneuvers deftly in the midst of a global economic meltdown, preventing E Corp's collapse by introducing E Coin.

E Coin is E Corp's digital currency solution to the banking collapse. Not only does it offer consumers an alternative to U.S. currency, it also becomes an *official* alternative currency when Price negotiates an E Coin loan program with the US Treasury Secretary ("pyth0n-pt1.p7z").

Price argues that, if the deal doesn't go through, Bitcoin, which he erroneously represents as Chinese-controlled, will take over. If that happens, he claims, "we will all be in a world of hell . . . With E Coin we control the ledger, and the mining servers. We are the authority."

So, despite the fact that credit cards are useless, mortgage payment records lost, massive protests continue at E Corp headquarters, and the US government refuses to bail it out, E Corp will become arguably even stronger after the attacks than before them.

What Is E Corp?

"People did this," Price tells Angela. "Whoever's behind this, they're just people" ("zer0-day.avi"). "This" is the fsociety hack intended to annihilate Evil Corp, and with it, many people's problems. He could just as well be talking about E Corp itself.

With this and similar dialogue, we can see that Phillip apparently understands the ontology—the existence—of social, political, and economic institutions. More specifically, he understands that *individuals* constitute these organizations. *Individuals*, therefore, are responsible for what they do. He also understands the power of hypostatization, which is the error of converting abstractions into concrete entities. We feel this power when, as Price tells Angela, "I have the weight of the biggest conglomerate in the world behind me." In other words, he has not simply the power of multitudes of individuals working together to sustain the company, he also knows that the public *conceives* of E Corp, for better or worse, as a kind of really existent entity. How is this possible?

We very easily talk about individual things, like the friend who's in town for a visit, a lost puppy seen wandering in the neighborhood, or the tree in the backyard. These we take to be really existent entities.

We can just as easily talk about Santa Claus, a woodland fairy, or the Loch Ness monster. These sorts of entities we don't take to be really existent—at least not by the time we reach a certain age. Instead, they are fictions of the imagination. Notice, however, in either category—really existent or fictitious entities—we're talking about individual things. What about abstract entities? Are they real like the tree in the backyard, or fictions like the Loch Ness monster?

We talk about abstractions just as easily as we talk about individuals. So, for example, we use mathematical formulas and the concept, number; we refer to the category, dog; or we agree with Elliot and Angela that Evil Corp was responsible for their parents' deaths. What, exactly, do we mean when we talk like this? What is the ontological status of these abstractions? Do they have any sort of objective existence?

We can put the problem in slightly different terms, in order to get at how the question arises in another way. I can write the Arabic numeral "1" on a piece of paper. It is a particular "1," but it is also a universal symbol for a quantity. Or again, I can look around the room and pick out my dog, Stewie. I can do the same for my other dogs Joe and H. I can then generalize to the concept, "dog." Here the move is from the particular to the general.

When, on the other hand, I begin with the general class or the universal number, I'm enlisting postulates that allow us to make, for example, comparisons between individual things. What, exactly, are these postulates? What is the reality of "dog," when individual dogs are lying about all over the world? Is "dog" lying about all over the world? That sounds ridiculous, and yet, we often ascribe real existence to universals.

Plato was convinced that universals are real. They are, he argues, the only way to explain what there is. In other words, the only way we recognize this or that dog is because Dog is real. Dog (the essence of dogs, or Dogness) makes possible the identification of particular dogs. Similarly, Good is real, since without it, we would not recognize individual good things and events. Plato calls these universals Forms.

The Forms are immutable. That means they are eternal, outside space and time, and immaterial—they don't degrade, as material things do. For Plato, then, the Forms exist in a realm entirely distinct from our own, but their nature allows us to access them through our rationality.

The world around us is in continual flux, so our senses provide us only with immediate, fleeting perceptions. Because of their nature, sensations are not concepts; they are not the apparatus we use to generalize *this* feeling of a fire's heat, *that* image of an apple's color, or *this* taste of a piece of chocolate. Sensations are always particularized. We don't feel general heat any more than we see general color. So also with our internal senses, such as the pain of a headache or the joy felt upon seeing a dear friend after a long absence.

A generalization can't be an object for sensation. It *is*, however, an object for reason, which allows us to generalize or think about generalities. Our reason alone moves to the general; our reason alone thereby fixes concepts. By our reason, then, albeit with great difficulty, we can get at the intelligible realm of the Forms.

Plato would have no problem, then, with our accounts of E Corp as a real entity, insofar as it participates in the Form of Corporation. (If the Forms are real, then there must be a Form of entities not yet discovered during Plato's time.) While Plato's explanation of universals is at least somewhat compelling, it does sound rather strange when we claim that it also explains things like E Corp.

Aristotle offers an alternative account of forms that alleviates some of Plato's theory's apparent strangeness, although it is not without its own difficulties. When Aristotle tells us that when we ask what there is ('What is being?'), we are asking, 'What is substance?' or 'What is beingness?' We can most easily identify individual substances, what Aristotle calls primary substances, or the basic existing entities.

According to Aristotle's account, everything else—everything that is not a primary substance—either inheres in, or is 'said of' a primary substance. Genus for example, is said of a species, which is said of a primary substance; these so-called secondary substances are means by which the latter are categorized. If we think about non-substances, on the other hand, we can readily see what Aristotle means by 'inhering in' a substance. The color blue, for example, does not exist independently of some object or other—it can't, in fact—but is inherent in it.

A primary substance—an individual—is an object of predication, but is not predicated of something else. Unless we are Yoda, we don't say, for example, "Paranoid is Elliot." In addition, a primary substance can receive contraries. Gideon can go, for example, from being the owner of a successful cybersecurity firm to being the former owner of a successful cybersecurity firm. Lastly, without a primary substance, there would be no properties. There is no blue without an object in which the color inheres.

Think of an individual thing as a combination of form and matter. This seems a reasonable way for Aristotle to bring Plato's Forms down to Earth. We see the form in the matter—matter takes form in individual objects, or form is immanent in matter to constitute individual objects.

What, then, is E Corp? It surely does not seem to be a primary substance. It's not a perceptible object. Consequently, it cannot be a candidate for classification under a species, which we know Aristotle takes to be a secondary substance. How, then, are we to make sense of it? Is it simply a name we give to a way or ways specific people have of interacting? We might get some traction on that front, since we could turn to Aristotle's ethical theory for guidance. The problem in that case, however, is that we're no longer talking about E Corp, but back to talking about individuals. It would seem, on Aristotle's view, at least, that E Corp is not an individual.

Is E Corp a Person?

Perhaps all is not lost for E Corp's ontological status. It does, after all, have the status of *legal* personhood. United States Code §1 asserts, "the words 'person' and 'whoever' include corporations, companies, associations, firms, partnerships, societies, and joint stock companies, as well as individuals" (Title 1—General Provisions). "The code is a consolidation and codification by subject matter of the general and permanent laws of the United States."

The practice of treating corporations as persons has, however, been around for much longer than these two rulings. In the US, as early as 1819, the Court held that corporations have a right to make and enforce contracts, just as persons do, and this designation became more fleshed out and solidified in subsequent rulings.

The 2010 US Supreme Court ruling extended this idea of the corporation as person in *Citizens United v. Federal Election Commission*. In *Citizens United*, the Court held that corporations and labor unions' First Amendment right of free speech allowed for unlimited spending on direct advocacy for or against political candidates. Another recent US Supreme Court case was 2014's *Burwell v. Hobby Lobby*. In that case, the Court decided that compelling corporations owned by religious individuals to provide contraception for female employees would violate the Religious Freedom Restoration Act.

A charitable view of corporate personhood as a legal fiction is that it serves as a mechanism for assigning rights and duties to organizations whose members may change over time.

Peter A. French offers three theories of the nature of a corporation: The Fiction Theory, which asserts that the corporation is a creation of the state. The Aggregate Theory "treats biological status as having legal priority and corporate existence as a contrivance for purposes of summary reference." Holders of this theory generally view corporate directors, executives, and stakeholders as the biological entities identified with the corporation, rather than the employees. Lastly, the Reality Theory views corporations not as legal subjects, but as a sociological entity the law recognizes. French's own view is that a corporation's organizational structure reveals the way decisions are made, thereby reflecting intentionality and so also moral responsibility.

In the most general sense of the word, corporations have been understood as collections of individuals united in one body. That "body" is the "corp" part of "corporation." It derives from the Latin, "corpus," meaning body. Etymologically, anyway, a corporation is on track to be conceived as an entity of the sort we have in mind when we think about individual things. Corporate status provides certain legal benefits that a partnership, for example, does not. If a partner dies, the partnership is thereby dissolved, but if a member of a corporation dies, the corporation lives on.

Perhaps the greatest benefit of corporate existence is that responsibility is diffused, sometimes almost to the point of evaporation, while simultaneously affording many rights extended to individuals in the Bill of Rights. For example, corporations are protected against warrantless search and seizure, and have the right to enter into contracts. Corporations can own property. As such, a corporation is considered a legal entity *independent* of the individuals that constitute it.

While it seems perfectly reasonable to grant personhood to corporations for efficiencies, such as taxes and complex transactions, and while it is also okay to protect individuals' rights to associate, the analogy of corporation to individual person eventually breaks down. Consider, for example, the fact that the US Supreme Court has yet to hold a corporation has the Fifth Amendment right against self-incrimination. Surely, that would be all but impossible to grant, unless the corporation's legal status is altered so as to be identified with, say, the CEO— the CEO just is the corporation, and vice versa. If that were the case, however, the legal purpose of the corporation would fall apart.

The problem of taking corporate personhood too literally appears particularly problematic in recent cases like the US Supreme Court ruling in *Citizens United* (2010) and *Hobby Lobby* (2014). In the former case, the individuals' right of free expression is amplified by the extension that is—like an additional limb—corporate personhood. In the latter ruling, a privately owned *company* was allowed to hold religious views. Yet corporations can't vote, can't hold office, can't ride with you in the carpool lane, can't take the Fifth—heck, they can't testify in court, period. Corporations don't have beliefs, feelings, attitudes, or reasons, at least not the way you and I do. How, then, can they be morally responsible?

The 1989 Exxon Valdez oil spill in Alaska that released millions of gallons of crude oil into the waters of Prince William Sound all but wiped out habitats for sea otters, salmon, seals, and sea birds. In 2010, BP Oil's Deepwater Horizon explosion in the Gulf of Mexico devastated the region's ecosystem and thousands of people's livelihoods. Eleven people who were working on the oil platform went missing and were never found. Researchers are still working to understand the marine spill's impact.

Criminal charges were brought against Pacific Gas and Electric, California's largest utility, after a 2010 pipeline explosion destroyed a suburban neighborhood and killed eight people. Nevertheless, unless the corporation's board members, executives, officers, and employees are convicted of a crime, no person goes to jail.

Each of these companies was held to account. Still we are unsatisfied. Why? Perhaps it's because we expect the individuals who run these corporations to make decisions that prioritize "doing good" over making a greater profit by cutting corners. Such individuals can be held liable for breaking the law or other malfeasance, as happened with Enron executives Kenneth L. Lay, Jeffrey K. Skilling, and Andrew S. Fastow. These and others at Enron were sentenced to prison for criminal acts, and Enron filed for bankruptcy. Enron itself didn't go to prison precisely because it does not have the requisite ontological or moral status for such a punishment.

Arthur Anderson, Enron's accounting firm, shredded Enron documents. It was charged with a crime. Arthur Anderson, however, is not a "natural" person, but rather a legal fiction. Anderson was charged with obstruction of justice, which involves *doing* and *intending*. A legal fiction simply can't *do* or *intend*. Only natural individuals can. A corporation can't go to jail. At the very least, this fact undermines the purpose of punishment, which is society's traditional response to certain wrongdoings. So, when individuals are arrested, as happened to E Corp executives, there is arguably only a partial fulfillment of moral responsibility.

The Moral Problem with Legal Personhood

A corporation is a legally distinct entity. Since this entity isn't real in the way an individual is real, we're hard pressed to find how that entity can truly be responsible—morally, at least—in the ways we hold individuals responsible. Granted, these rights are circumscribed, yet, the scope extends too far to adequately accord with at least one version of morality rooted in the dignity of persons: free, rational, and self-legislating individuals.

Immanuel Kant argues that moral action is evaluated by the motivation that drives the act (*Groundwork of the Metaphysics of Morals*). More specifically, Kant thinks a moral action is one motivated by a respect for duty, rather than, say, an inclination to get something out of the effort. In other words, outcomes don't bear on the morality of the act.

Moreover, one whose actions merely accord with duty, but are not motivated by it, don't get moral points: "it is not enough that it *conform* to the law, it must be also be done *for its own sake*" (pp. 5–6). The root of this respect for duty in Kant's moral theory is human rationality. Duty is, according to Kant, the "necessity of an action from respect for the law" (p. 16). As it is reason that generates the moral law, when we recognize our obligation to that law, we effectively respect ourselves as rational beings. Duty is, then, an internally generated constraint upon us.

One way Kant articulates the moral law is as follows: "so act as to treat humanity, whether in your own person or in that of another, never merely as a means, but also always as an end in itself" (p. 45). The inherent worth or dignity of human beings demands my respect and recognition that I am limited in how I interact with people when pursuing some goal or other.

The primary problem with the morality of corporate personhood is that it is simply impossible to respect a non-human entity in the way the moral law demands. This is, perhaps, an explanation for why we find corporate personhood deeply dissatisfying.

All this brings us back to E Corp, and in particular, Angela and Elliot's desire for justice. For our part, it would seem the aversion to E Corp's practices is a pre-reflective rejection of viewing corporations as persons, bound up as E Corp's persona is with real life stories of corporate misdeeds. In our frustration to hold someone accountable for terrible conduct, we look for the responsible party—a person who has used us poorly, who, directly or indirectly, has not treated us with dignity. Upon examination, however, we find there really is no moral "who" of E Corp, just many individuals led by a well-protected CEO.

Take, for example, Angela's quest to find the person or persons responsible for deciding what happened at E Corp's New Jersey factories. Angela goes to Terry Colby's house to offer him a deal: if he testifies against E Corp for covering up the illegal waste dump, she'll make sure the evidence against him disappears, thereby ensuring his freedom. He rejects her in a most vulgar way. "If you don't take this deal," Angela replies, "you'll become like me. Sure, maybe you'll live in this house, maybe you'll have money. But even if your expensive lawyers find a way to get you off, people will still think that you're guilty. Losing everyone's respect. The respect of people you know, and the people you don't. It's a shitty feeling. Trust me" ("v1ew-s0urce.flv").

Just how much Angela's self-worth has been compromised is unclear, though there are scenes at the end of Season One and in Season Two that suggest she believes she's regained some of it through her rise at E Corp. It looks as if she falls for Philip Price's interest in her, even as she doubts his motivations. Consider, for example, her initial surprise at his dinner invitation, and then her apparent disappointment when she arrives at the restaurant to find him with two other men.

Later Colby offers her his own advice, along with a job at E Corp ("M1RR0R1NG.qt"). "If you want to change things," he tells her, "perhaps you should try from within." Within the belly of the beast is where Angela will interact with actual moral agents, those who are not persons for legal purposes only. It is within her role at E Corp that she meets two E Corp executives responsible for the cover up of the epoxy resin waste spill that killed her mother (as protestors stake out the restaurant where the group is having dinner).

After the men leave, Price drops his bombshell. "They were both in the room with Colby when they made that grave error, covering up the leak in your home town. Ordinary men, capable of extraordinary things." Of course, he also discloses that they have "engaged in some nasty insider trading" ("k3rnel-pan1c.ksd").

For this reason he provides Angela with "enough evidence to put them away for years." She knew *someone* or a specific group was ultimately responsible and has wanted to find and punish *them*. Indeed, the two executives are subsequently arrested when Angela turns over the material to her lawyer, but she remains dubious, and not simply because Price is not someone to trust. She was initially pleased to see Colby wearing an ankle bracelet while under house arrest in "3xpl0its.wmv," which leads us to believe she thinks she's on the right track. It's because, even with their arrests, there is a moral imbalance.

We can see that E Corp is neither an Aristotelian individual nor a moral agent—without intentions and reason, it can't be. At the same time, it's a legal person that can be held criminally liable. A tension results, then, particularly when we humans, who have created the concept of legal personhood, typically consider crimes to be immoral acts. *Mr. Robot* helps draw out this tension by focusing on the individual humans caught up—intentionally or accidentally—in the ensuing drama.

15
Reset Virtues

DARCI DOLL

Hello, friend. It's just you and I right now. Elliot and Mr. Robot aren't around and we can speak freely.

We've been with Elliot long enough to know that he's different from most people. He lies, steals, hacks, invades privacy, does drugs, and has a mental illness that he's allowed to go untreated. This mental illness causes him to disassociate from his actions, hallucinate, break the law, become violent, invent friends and alter personalities. You're probably wondering: is Elliot a hero, an anti-hero, the villain? As products of his imaginations, it's natural that we would want to better understand the world of which we're a part.

In examining Elliot's behaviors and motivations, it may be surprising to find that many of his characteristics are consistent with virtues identified by Aristotelian, or Aristotelian-inspired, virtue ethics. Elliot has habituated himself to use his wisdom, skills, and proper moral motivations to bring about change that will help others, specifically with respect to the social environment that shapes individuals and their potential. More impressively, Elliot appears to have also passed these traits on to his alter personality, Mr. Robot, and to us, his unnamed friends.

Mr. Robot says, "The world is a dangerous place . . . not because of those who do evil, but because of those who look on and do nothing." Does Elliot's response to this statement put him on the side of either virtue or vice?

logic-bOmb

The roots of the codes and programming with which Elliot hacks the world may be traced back to Athens in the fourth century B.C. when the philosopher Aristotle developed logic; a system through which we can evaluate the reasonableness of an argument. Much in the ways Elliot describes programming as setting boundaries for possible responses or interactions, logic creates similar rules for arguments.

You've probably noticed that Elliot often speaks about people analogously to computers; he discusses programs, vulnerabilities in code, bugs, daemons as part of how he sees humans. Often, he juxtaposes this with a comment about how he's not normal, how he doesn't function the way other humans do. Yet he's not too far off from an Aristotelian correlation between logic and the human condition.

unm4sk

According to Aristotle, all people crave *eudaimonia*. We want to be the best versions of our selves; we crave excellence and flourishing and we crave the type of happiness that comes along with those things.

We are attracted to things that we perceive as being good for us, the things that we think will help us attain *Eudaimonia*, and we avoid the things that we think are contrary to it.

We are, however, products of our environments, surroundings, influenced by people around us. It's possible that we may be mistaken about what's actually in our own best interest. For Aristotle this means that we aren't born good or bad; we become either good or bad based on the decisions we make and the way that we shape ourselves. Because of this Aristotle didn't recommend that we do what feels best to us; rather, he said we need to acquire practical wisdom to help us identify the difference between what's actually good versus what may only appear to be good because of how our perception has been shaped throughout our lives. He is essentially requiring that we attain knowledge, wisdom, and take a logically ordered approach to it.

Since we all desire *eudaimonia,* we need to first understand the world around us, the things which help humans flourish, those which interfere with or corrupt flourishing. Once we understand this, we are to act in ways consistent with those traits until they become habit; once they're so habituated that we have programmed ourselves to be of good character. People who have achieved this are virtuous; those who cultivate the opposite are either non-virtuous or vicious.

da3mOns

Knowing what you know about Elliot, I presume you'll categorize him as vicious. He breaks laws, he violates people's privacy. He uses illegal drugs and avoids the prescription drugs that are meant to keep him mentally healthy. Then we have Mr. Robot; a mysterious component of Elliot whose intentions are suspect. At best guess (we're in no position to make an official diagnosis, after all) Mr. Robot is an identity distinct from the person we know as Elliot.

Mr. Robot is who Elliot refers to as the mastermind; the one who was willing to blow up buildings and risk lives in taking down Steel Mountain and the paper back-ups in the E Corp storage building. At best, we can say that Elliot and Mr. Robot are acting in ways that they think are best, but they're incorrect about that; the end result is that they aren't what Aristotle had in mind when he spoke of cultivating virtues.

decOd3d

While it's true that Mr. Robot appears to be evidence that Elliot may have a version of malignant Dissociative Identity Disorder (DID), Elliot has modified his internal programming to try to minimize the malicious codes of these other components of his personality. When Elliot becomes aware of the true identity of Mr. Robot, he takes efforts to ensure that Mr. Robot's ability to do damage is minimized if not eliminated. He tries to subvert the plans, he allows himself to get arrested, restricts himself to a strict analog regime inspired by his mother while he's in prison, ODs on Adderall. He does everything within his power to stop Mr. Robot from harming people. Elliot is set on taking control and doing the right thing, even when Elliot believes Tyrell may be another identity Elliot endures physical harm to try to stop the damage of Stage Two of the hack

m4ster-s1ave

This is a mark of someone who is trying to use their sense of morally good character to condition and habituate, to control, their personal vices. Elliot's task is more difficult than others because he has to create this conditioning when he's in absence of control, however; that doesn't stop him from trying.

Elliot is embodying the Aristotelian idea of virtue ethics; he uses his wisdom to identify what's right, and alter his habits and environment to align with that. Upon learning the full scope of the consequences of the 5/9 hack, Elliot said he was, "okay with being on the hook; I'll own it all. Maybe it'll even stop Darlene from doing some crazy shit. At this rate, she's going to end up just like Gideon."

While Elliot believed in the principles behind the 5/9 hack, he wasn't willing to let innocent people suffer for his sins. He was willing to confess to Ray and risk legal repercussions. Likewise, he was willing to risk his personal well-being to expose Ray's website once he knew what Ray's business entailed. Ray commented that Elliot unexpectedly became his savior by freeing him from the weight of the website. Elliot wanted to save the world; he utilized everything at his disposal, even unleashing Mr. Robot, to make that possible. When he realized the extent to which innocent people were hurt because of his decisions, he was willing to put himself on the line to rectify it.

As Elliot is contemplating playing Mr. Robot for control of their existence, Leon asks whether Elliot dreams; if he really wants to be *here* in the cosmic sense. He says:

LEON: Do you dream, Elliot? You scraping so hard like you ain't never asked yourself this before. I said, do you want to be here right now? And I don't mean here here, but I mean here in a cosmic sense, bro. Like existence could be beautiful, or it could be ugly, but that's on you.

ELLIOT: How do I know which one's for me?

LEON: Dream. You got to find out the future you're fighting for. Sometimes you've got to close your eyes and really envision that shit, bro. If you like it, then it's beautiful. If you don't? Then you might as well fade the fuck out right now.

m1rrOr1ng

Leon's message is Aristotelian in the sense that it's the question of whether you're willing to do the work to cultivate the habits that will best enable you to attain *eudaimonia* by first identifying what that lifestyle looks like. Then, the burden falls on you to decide whether to make it happen.

Happiness, excellence, flourishing are all choices and our commitment to them is demonstrated in the lives we live. In reflecting on Leon's question Elliot concludes that the life he's striving for is one that involves connections to the people he cares for, making amends for the wrongs he's committed in the past, "A future filled with friends and family." And he's included you, too, in this world he's always wanted, one that he "would like very much to fight for."

This is where we can start to see that Elliot has been focusing on his perceived good without actually visualizing and examining what is actually good. His 5/9 attack was intended to save the world; upon its execution Elliot realized that the costs may not have been worth the benefits. He's reluctant to carry it to completion. He's presented himself with the opportunity for annihilation; he or Mr. Robot will be able to exist, but not both.

He now has to identify which of these realities is preferable—which one is going to help him be the best version of himself. Undoubtedly there are times where Elliot believes Mr. Robot has some superior skills; other times he calls him into question. But now's the time for him to decide what is best and then take the actions that will enable him to habituate the character traits and actions that will allow that to become an actuality.

d3bug

While in prison, Elliot believes that annihilation is the only answer. He has identified what the good life looks like and cannot see the possibility of achieving this while Mr. Robot exists. Krista warns him of the danger of this; that there's an integrated legitimate existence between Elliot and Mr. Robot. Before he's released from prison, Elliot realizes that Krista is correct: to destroy part of his personality, his existence, is too extreme.

He has to find a way to balance the two identities and make them co-operate. We see the symbiotic relationship where Mr. Robot protects Elliot from physical and emotional pain and we see Elliot finally begin to understand the importance of Mr. Robot when he says, "Mr. Robot was a part of me that I created because of my pain. So now we have a chance to start again. Our handshake negotiated us as partners." When he's willing to accept the value of Mr. Robot, he's able to see that what the world needs is Elliot as a leader, and Mr. Robot is the prophet who will help him achieve that.

Elliot has begun to understand that he can still use his unique sets of skills, Mr. Robot, and his imaginary skills to bring about the positive changes that the world needs. He still believes that people can't flourish, will continue to be enslaved, unless he finishes what he started. Evil Corp still has too much ownership of the world. What he's learned, however, is that he has to find the balance between himself and Mr. Robot. He needs to condition and habituate Mr.

Robot as well to ensure that together their behaviors are consistent with virtue and the life he's envisioned for himself.

succ3ssOr

Ray told Elliot that what he has, the voices he hears, can be divinity if he lets them. And this, my friend, is where we can see our role.

We are the if/then conditional programming that Elliot has created to help keep himself in good behavior. When he needs help, he asks us. When he's uncertain of reality, he looks to us for confirmation. Elliot is aware that without us, he can't be certain of ensuring good behavior. He can't keep the balance with Mr. Robot functioning.

I started out by asking whether Elliot was a villain, hero, anti-hero, virtuous, or vicious. But, my friend, those are not the questions. We're here to help Elliot fight for the future he wants; we're here to help him save the world. We're here to create the environment that lets him be our virtuous anti-hero.

VI

Is Any of
It Real?

16
On-keeping-everybOdy-1n-the-d4rk.docx

DON FALLIS

Mr. Robot depicts a great hidden war between *epistemic* adversaries. In this war, the combatants do not (at least usually) shoot at each other or try to blow each other up. Instead, hackers and cybersecurity experts attack what the other guy *knows* about the world.

The type of epistemic adversary that philosophers tend to focus on is the *deceiver*. (Remember Descartes's "malicious demon of the utmost power and cunning who has employed all his energies in order to deceive me.") The goal of the deceiver is to cause people to have *false* beliefs about the world.

Elliot Alderson and his friends at fsociety certainly engage in a lot of deception. For instance, they put Terry Colby's IP address into the DAT file in order to frame him for the DDoS attack on "Evil Corp." They lie to several employees in order to gain access to Steel Mountain, going so far as to create a fake identity for Elliot in Wikipedia. Indeed, every time he logs into someone else's account using a hacked password, Elliot is arguably deceiving the computer system about who he is.

More often than not, however, hackers and cybersecurity experts are simply trying to *keep everybody in the dark*. In other words, they just want us to *not* have true beliefs about the world. For instance, cybersecurity firms, such as Allsafe, want to keep hackers in the dark about our passwords and our data. And hackers want to keep the rest of us in the dark about what they are up to.

Elliot, in particular, keeps all sorts of people in the dark about all sorts of things. The aim of his 5/9 attack is to destroy all of the records of debt in the world and, thus, to prevent Evil Corp from knowing what people owe. Elliot even keeps the audience in the dark (for half of the second season!) about the fact that he has been in jail. (At the end of "eps2.5_h4nd-shake.sme," Elliot feels compelled to apologize to us, "I'm sorry for not telling you everything. But I needed this in order to get better. Please don't be mad too long. This will be the last time I keep things from you. I promise.") But most interestingly, Elliot frequently keeps *himself* in the dark about exactly what is going on, such as what happened to Tyrell on the night of the 5/9 attack and what "Stage Two" is.

Defining Our Terms

The first step toward understanding *deception* and *keeping people in the dark* is to define our terms. In his Socratic dialogues, Plato famously offered definitions of concepts, such as knowledge, justice, and love. Philosophers still debate about how to best define these concepts.

Philosophers are largely in agreement, though, about the concept of deception. You deceive someone if you intentionally cause her to have a false belief. However, keeping people in the dark turns out to be a trickier concept. Several definitions have been proposed.

The Harvard University philosopher Sissela Bok has written an influential book on *Lying* and another influential book on *Secrets*. In the second book, she gives a definition of what it means to *keep a secret*. And keeping X a secret from someone is essentially the same as keeping her in the dark about X. According to Bok, "to keep a secret from someone . . . is to block information about it or evidence of it from reaching that person, and to do so intentionally."

Bok's definition looks pretty good. In almost all cases, we do keep people in the dark by intentionally concealing information from them. The most obvious example is when we wear a mask in order to hide our identity. In addition to being a symbol of anarchy, the stylized mask of Guy Fawkes, the guy who tried to blow up Parliament, conceals who the members of the hacker group Anonymous are. The "Monopoly Man" mask serves the same purpose for the members and supporters of fsociety.

Many more sophisticated examples of concealment can also be found in *Mr. Robot*. For instance, in "eps1.9_zer0-day.avi," the members of fsociety throw an "End of the World" party, but it's not just a celebration of the success of the 5/9 hack. It is, more importantly, a way to keep the authorities in the dark about who's responsible for the hack. By getting a bunch of people to mill around the arcade, the members of fsociety are able to cover-up any evidence of their identities that they might have left behind.

> ROMERO: Well, this place is a petri dish now.

> MOBLEY: Yup, I'd say we got enough fingerprints everywhere.

Indeed, the 5/9 attack itself falls under Bok's definition. Destroying information is clearly one way of concealing it (forever).

Moreover, you typically have to conceal information or your intended victim will notice that something is amiss and will not remain in the dark. This is why, early in "eps1.5_br4ve-trave1er.asf," Elliot fails to break into the computer system of the prison holding Shayla's drug supplier Vera. Because she had too little time to work on it, the malware that Darlene wrote for Elliot is detected by the computer system.

Yet another important aspect of Bok's definition is that, just like deceiving someone, keeping someone in the dark is an *intentional* act. If you accidentally conceal information from someone, you are not keeping her in the dark in the sense that philosophers have been focused on. For instance, as Agent DiPierro discovers in "eps2.1_k3rnel-pan1c.ksd,"

Romero's mother concealed evidence of fsociety's activities, including the flier for the "End of the World" party. But she didn't do this intentionally. Romero's mother was simply wrapping glasses with whatever paper was lying around because she was planning to move.

Counterexamples

But despite its many attractive features, Bok's definition can't be correct. While it's a standard way to keep someone in the dark, actively concealing information is not actually *required* to keep someone in the dark. Passively withholding information is sometimes sufficient. For instance, as the contemporary philosopher Thomas Carson points out, "a lawyer keeps her client in the dark if she fails to inform him that a certain course of action she is advising him to take is likely to result in his being the subject of a lawsuit."

One of the more oblivious characters in *Mr. Robot* actually provides us with the same sort of counterexample to Bok's definition. For quite a while, Elliot keeps his therapist Krista in the dark about the fact that he has hacked into her accounts and is observing the private details of her life. And he doesn't have to conceal any information in order to prevent Krista from finding out about what he is up to. Elliot just has to keep his mouth shut (which he does until the end of "eps1.6_v1ew-s0urce.flv"). Krista is too absorbed with her own problems to notice that the patient sitting in her office might be an epistemic adversary.

Admittedly, Elliot does conceal information to keep Krista in the dark about *certain* facts. In "eps1.0_hellofriend.mov," in order to protect her, Elliot forces the "dickhead" Lenny who is cheating on his wife to break up with Krista. And it seems to be part of Elliot's deal with Lenny that Lenny not tell Krista about Elliot's role in the breakup. By making this deal, Elliot is blocking information from getting to Krista. Thus, on Bok's definition, he is keeping her in the dark about his meddling in her life in this way. But since Elliot (at least initially) keeps Krista in the dark about his hacking her accounts just by withholding information, Bok's definition incorrectly rules out some instances of keeping people in the dark.

Chisholming Our Way to a Definition

It would be easy to tweak Bok's definition in order to deal with the aforementioned counterexample. Basically, we could say that you keep someone in the dark if you intentionally conceal *or* withhold information from her. However, this revised Bok definition can't be correct either.

Elliot keeps people in the dark about all sorts of things. But he does not keep people in the dark whenever keeps his mouth shut about something. For instance, in addition to not telling people that he is behind the 5/9 attack, Elliot also doesn't go around telling people what he had for breakfast every morning. Moreover, this is intentional; even Elliot knows that it would be boorish to blather on about all of the trivial details of his life. But nevertheless, we would not want to say that he is keeping people in the dark about his morning rituals.

We could try to further tweak the revised Bok definition in order to deal with this new counterexample. Philosophers (at www.philosophicallexicon.com) have coined the term "chisholming" to refer to (and make fun of) this sort of practice. The Brown University philosopher Roderick Chisholm (1916–1999) was famous for starting with a simple definition of some concept and then proposing ever more complicated definitions in order to deal with potential counterexamples.

But even if we could chisholm our way out of this problem, I think that focusing on concealing and withholding information is actually taking us down the wrong path. While concealing and withholding information are common ways to keep someone in the dark, they are not *constitutive* of keeping someone in the dark. It is what happens to someone's knowledge, rather than what happens to some information, that determines whether or not she has been kept in the dark. So, what *is* the right way to define keeping someone in the dark? I think that it is just a slight variation on our definition of deception.

Negative Deception

The most common way to deceive someone is to provide her with misleading information. For instance, you might create fake evidence as Elliot does with the DAT file in "eps1.0_hellofriend.mov." Or you might simply lie as when Elliot claims to be billionaire Sam Sepiol (the "Next Zuckerberg") in "ps1.4_3xpl0its.wmv." But we don't *define* deception in terms of intentionally providing misleading information. Instead, we say that you deceive someone if you intentionally cause her to have a false belief. In other words, we define deception in terms of the (suboptimal) knowledge state that is brought about rather than in terms of the method of bringing about that knowledge state. In a similar vein, we should just say that you keep someone in the dark if you intentionally cause her *not* to have a true belief.

Ironically enough, this definition was originally proposed by Roderick Chisholm. This is a case where (I believe that) he actually got the definition correct right off the bat, with no chisholming. The only catch is that Chisholm was not actually proposing a definition of the concept of keeping people in the dark. Instead, he was just trying to distinguish two different types of deception. Chisholm's idea was that "positive deception" results in a false belief whereas "negative deception" merely results in the lack of a true belief. Basically, he wanted to treat keeping people in the dark as a type of deception.

Most philosophers think that this was a mistake on Chisholm's part. There are important differences between the two concepts. In particular, there seems to be something wrong on its face with deceiving someone. For instance, even if it was justified by the larger goals of fsociety's revolution, and even if he did do all sorts of other horrible stuff, there is still something icky about making people think that Colby was involved in the DDoS attack on Evil Corp when he wasn't. By contrast, there doesn't seem to be anything intrinsically wrong with keeping people in the dark. For instance, Krista has every right to keep patients in the dark about the details of her personal life. Elliot violates her privacy by breaking into her accounts even if his motivation is to help her.

Moreover, keeping people in the dark is not just permissible. It's often a good thing. And *not* keeping people in the dark can be a bad thing. In "eps2.3_logic-b0mb.hc," Tyrell's wife Joanna orders her henchman Mr. Sutherland to kill the parking lot attendant who found Tyrell's SUV, but to paralyze him first. ("We let him die with answers. Otherwise we're nothing but ruthless murderers.") Despite the justification she offers, it doesn't seem like Joanna is doing the parking lot attendant any favors by *not* keeping him in the dark about why he is dying.

But even if Chisholm was wrong about keeping people in the dark being a type of deception, he still came up with a pretty good definition of the concept.

The Paradox of Self-Deception

So, you keep someone in the dark if you leave her without a true belief. In most instances, it is clear how this can be accomplished. Namely, you simply conceal (or withhold) the relevant information from her. But there is one instance of keeping someone in the dark in *Mr. Robot* that is a little hard to explain. Elliot keeps *himself* in the dark about a number of things: about what happened to Tyrell on the night of the 5/9 attack, about his being sent to jail, and about what "Stage 2" is. How is this possible?

Admittedly, it is possible to keep yourself in the dark about some things. Spoilers written in code are an obvious example. In "eps2.9pyth0n-pt1.p7z," Mr. Robot uses the ROT-13 algorithm to decode a secret message. But this very simple cipher is more commonly used to post information (such as a description of part of a movie or a TV series) on a blog so that people will not be able to read the information if they do not want to read the information. Thus, you can keep yourself in the dark about how the second season of *Mr. Robot* ends simply by *not* replacing each letter in the blog post by the letter that is thirteen letters away in the alphabet.

But avoiding spoilers is a case where you *start out* in the dark. For instance, you don't initially have any idea about how the second season of *Mr. Robot* ends. So, you just have to prevent yourself from getting information that would give you such knowledge. But what if you already have a true belief on the topic that you want to keep yourself in the dark about? For instance, Elliot knows (or at least knew) what happened to Tyrell on the night of the 5/9 attack. After all, he was with Tyrell that night. Thus, simply withholding information from himself is not enough to keep himself in the dark. It is not sufficient for Elliot to prevent his knowledge state from getting better. Elliot has to make his knowledge state *worse*. In other words, he has to *deceive himself*. Thus, in order to explain how Elliot can keep himself in the dark, we have to confront what philosophers call the *Paradox of Self-Deception*.

Self-deception seems to be a fairly common phenomenon. For instance, Angela arguably deceives herself when she believes that Evil Corp hired her for her corporate skills and abilities. When he first offered her the job in "eps1.8_m1rr0r1ng.qt," Colby told her that she was "relentless and smart, and that combination is very valuable to a lot of important people." And that's what she ultimately chooses to believe. It couldn't possibly have been that they just needed her help to get the Washington Township lawsuit (the one involving the toxic gas leak that killed her mother) settled!

But it's not immediately clear how self-deception can possibly happen. It is hard enough to get someone else not to believe something that she currently believes. How can you get yourself not to believe something that you currently believe when *you know* that you are trying to get yourself not to believe it?

One strategy that a few philosophers have used to try to resolve this paradox is to posit two (or more) independent centers of agency in the same person. In other words, different parts of a person's mind are distinct agents, each with their own desires, goals, beliefs, and intentions. What happens in self-deception then is that one of these agents deceives another one of these agents. And this is no more paradoxical than when one person deceives another person.

Even though it resolves the paradox, most philosophers now think that this approach doesn't work so well for run-of-the-mill self-deception involving people, such as Angela, who don't have split personalities. But this "split personality" approach works perfectly for explaining how *Elliot* can keep himself in the dark. His mind clearly does have two independent centers of agency. There is the Elliot part and there is the Mr. Robot part. And it is the Mr. Robot part of Elliot that keeps the Elliot part of Elliot in the dark about what happened to Tyrell on the night of the 5/9 attack.

Now, this explanation of how Elliot keeps himself in the dark might appear to conflict with what happens in "eps2.2_init1.asec." Elliot and Mr. Robot play chess in order to see who will take over complete control of Elliot's mind. However, it turns out that there is no winner. All of the games end in a stalemate. But if Mr. Robot can keep Elliot in the dark about what "Stage 2" is, why couldn't he keep Elliot in the dark about what his next move will be and win the game?

Here's what I think is going on: What leads to the stalemate is not just that Mr. Robot and Elliot are evenly matched. Two evenly matched players can beat each other in any given game. What leads to the stalemate is that they are the *very same* player. Since they are using the same "processor," each of them can simulate the other in order to figure out what the next move will be. And even though Mr. Robot *can* keep Elliot in the dark about particular facts, this ability can't help him to win a game of chess. Unlike with poker (or conspiracies to hack large corporations), there is no hidden information in a game of chess.

The Python Approach

I hope I've convinced you that the concept of keeping people in the dark is not *just* of philosophical interest. Unless we want to end up like Krista, we need to be able to keep unethical hackers, evil corporations, and dispassionate governments in the dark about what we're up to.

We also need to be worried about unethical hackers, evil corporations, and dispassionate governments keeping us in the dark about what they're up to. After all, they might even be using the *Python Approach* (named after the snake and not the programming language). That is, they might be trying to hide the fact that they are after us. As Agent DiPierro says in "eps2.9_pyth0n-pt2.p7z" about the leader of fsociety, "It was imperative that we got him before he knew we were getting him."

Since the war between hackers and cybersecurity experts is heating up on the IRL network as well as on the USA network, it is important for all of us to understand what it is to keep people in the dark, how we can keep other people in the dark, and how we can prevent others from keeping us in the dark. *Mr. Robot* can be a useful testbed for this important project in applied epistemology.

17
Our Lying Eyes

Mia Wood

Elliot Alderson, an engineer at Allsafe Cybersecurity, has prodigious hacking skills. He uses these skills to right moral wrongs. He turns a pedophile in, despite the offender's attempt to bribe him into keeping silent. He forces his therapist's boyfriend to break up with her after learning the man is a serial adulterer with no real feelings for the women he betrays—and takes the adulterer's dog for good measure ("eps1.0_hellofriend.mov"). After all, the man was cruel to the pup.

By his own admission, however, Elliot is an unreliable narrator. "Hello, friend" is the first line of dialogue in *Mr. Robot*. His voiceover continues, "You're only in my head. We have to remember that." He then goes on to disclose what he calls a major secret: there is a conspiracy "bigger than all of us." These are men so powerful they can hide their misdeeds from our scrutiny. They are, Elliot tells us, invisible.

Elliot's dubious reliability is exhibited by two extended sequences in Season 1.0 and Season 2.0: Elliot believes he's interacting with someone named Mr. Robot, and we believe Elliot is living at his mother's house while laying low during the fallout from the E Corp hack.

So, we're faced with a problem. Elliot's grasp on reality is shaky, and the way he navigates the world is shaped by social anxiety, depression, and probably autism. He experiences vivid hallucinations. He takes medication—or should, anyway—to control them. His problem is compounded by a burgeoning morphine addiction, which further alters his interactions. Given all this, how can he—and we—know anything at all, let alone make good decisions about how to act?

Still, we want to believe Elliot. The sensitive introvert is a sympathetic character with apparently decent intentions. It also seems as if there's good reason to believe him when he worries over Evil Corp's domination of so many aspects of our lives. The idea of a few powerful people "secretly" running the world doesn't sound so far-fetched. From the Enron scandal, first publicized in 2001, to the unethical conduct by members of a handful of banks "too big to fail," to the distressing fact of income inequality, it surely appears that power and wealth are consolidated into too few hands.

Corporations have long been perceived as getting away with polluting the environment, and poisoning people. Financial settlements don't seem proportionate to the injustices done. For its part, Evil Corp owns chemical plants and media companies, manufactures computers, phones, and tablets, and runs an enormous banking services division that includes mortgages and a large percentage of the global consumer credit industry.

We root for Elliot, who is impassioned about this injustice, about people controlling our lives so effectively that we don't realize it until it's too late. As he says, they "play God without permission." Only a rare few—Ayn Rand followers, for example—would think this conduct is morally acceptable, let alone conduct we should promote. Consequently, we take the leap with Elliot. We root for him.

Elliot's Perceptions

We see what Elliot sees. We hear what Elliot hears. We share his perceptions. They are initially and often consistent, and so they don't at first provoke any doubts about his ideas—our ideas. For example, Elliot sees a man on the subway. Later, that man appears again. Elliot finds a file on the Evil Corp server named fsociety00.dat, and a message commanding the reader to leave the malware hidden: "LEAVE ME HERE." Shortly thereafter, he meets Mr. Robot, so named because of a patch on the man's jacket. Elliot is then recruited to help implement the plan to destroy all of E Corp's debt records —"Evil Corp," the company responsible for Elliot's father's death. Elliot believes that fsociety has planted malware in Evil Corp's server. He also believes that Mr. Robot is the mastermind behind fsociety.

Over the course of the first season, Elliot and fsociety come to believe their actions have brought E Corp to its knees. In Season 2.0, however, we learn that E Corp's CEO, Phillip Price, has been conspiring with the Chinese Minister of Security to take control over US currency ("init_5.fve"). Similarly, when we claimed to know that Elliot was spending time with his friend, Leon, we thought the two were hanging out together in a diner and on the basketball court. What we didn't know was that Elliot had been in jail for the past eighteen months, having pled guilty to hacking into Krista's ex-boyfriend's digital world and taking his dog. Because the pup was valued at over one thousand dollars, "stealing" her was a felony.

Between Elliot's basic perceptual problems and the deceptive machinations of very powerful people, can Elliot—or we—be certain of anything?

Making Sense of Perception

Throughout almost the entire first season, when we're with Elliot, we see and hear only what he perceives. Everything hangs together pretty well, despite Elliot's own original caution about the reliability of his mind.

According to the philosophical theory known as *empiricism*, we get our beliefs about the world from the evidence of our senses. We acquire knowledge by seeing, touching, hearing, smelling, and tasting. For empiricists such as John Locke and George Berkeley, it is sense experience alone that provides the direct material for our ideas. On the empiricists' account of idea formation, we can't ask for anything more.

As Locke tells us in his *Essay Concerning Human Understanding*, the mind is a "white paper" on which sensory experience is written, a space furnished by empirically derived ideas. Without experience, he concludes, there would be no "ideas," the mental objects of thought. So, if an organ of sense doesn't function, such as eyes or ears, we won't have any sight ideas or sound ideas; if there is an absence of any object, that is, if we go through life without certain experiences, we won't have the corresponding ideas.

Even our ideas produced by reflection, derived from the operations of our minds, are really, says Locke, derived from sensation. When, for example, we begin to reflect on the ideas we have, we observe modes of thinking, such as remembering and judging. While these perceptions spring from the mind, we come to awareness of them because they work on ideas derived from sensation. Hence, they are, practically speaking, parasitic upon the experience we get through our senses.

Berkeley takes what looks like a similar approach to idea formation. Ideas, he asserts, are collections of sensations. The idea of an apple is a collection of various sensations, such as sweetness, crunchiness, roundness, and so forth. On the face of it, we might wonder what difference there is between these two empiricist accounts of ideas, Locke's and Berkley's.

There is in fact a huge difference between the two. Locke claims that our ideas are copies of objects existing independently of our ideas of them. There really are objects out there in the world, and we become aware of their existence and their qualities by perceiving them using our senses. Berkeley maintains that there are no material objects: there are only clusters of perceptions. Only perceptions exist.

Locke believes there is a world of objects which exist independently of the mind. So, for Locke, it is quite easy to explain how there can be perceptual illusions. Through the first seven-and-a-half episodes of Season 1.0, Elliot experiences Mr. Robot as an actual person, and we experience events largely through Elliot's eyes. The most we can do is wonder about the veracity of those events. Once Angela and Darlene—in "eps1.8_m1rr0r1ng.qt"—question his perception, it seems clear he's been mistaken. Sometimes something goes wrong with our perceptions, and that means they don't accurately inform us about the world of material objects.

For most of us, Locke's account seems to be reasonable: our ideas are caused by the way objects affect us. Berkeley argues, however, that such a position opens us up to unresolvable doubt. The question that arises is how we know that our ideas match their objects. Can we know there is a world external to our minds, and if so, can we know its nature if we are ultimately only acquainted with our own ideas? With access only to the mental objects called ideas, it seems as if a chasm opens up between them and any material reality. Locke himself seems to struggle with this possibility when he asserts, "Whatsoever the mind perceives *in itself*, or is the immediate object of perception, thought, or understanding, that I call *idea*." According to Berkeley, however, since we have access only to our ideas, we can't talk meaningfully about anything else.

Only Ideas Exist

In his *Treatise Concerning the Principles of Human Knowledge*, Berkeley argues that it doesn't make any sense to claim that ideas are distinct from their objects. Think about it this way: that apple idea consists of a collection or bundle of sensations. If you think the apple itself exists independently of our idea of it, you have to show what it is *independently* of the idea.

When you begin to describe the object, you simply begin describing the sensations you have. Perhaps you also picture an apple. All that is just what it is to have an idea. It's not as if you can take your apple idea and set it down next to an apple for comparison. Even if you could, you'd just have another idea. As Berkeley tells us, contrary to Locke, ideas don't resemble *objects* in an external world: "an idea can be like nothing but another idea."

So, when you and I watch *Mr. Robot*, and we see and hear what Elliot sees and hears, we're having ideas. There's no *additional* standpoint we can take to talk meaningfully about those objects existing *independently* of our perceptions. Indeed, this is precisely the difficulty Elliot himself has—is he really having a conversation with Mr. Robot, is there really an object, a human being, standing opposite him?

It'a All in the Perception

Berkeley thinks that objects are indeed real, but they are nothing more than clusters of sense perceptions, or in the language of eighteenth-century philosophers, "ideas." Objects are not material things independent of the mind. If we think that objects exist "out there," independent of our perceptions of them, we go astray.

Berkeley, who was a Bishop in the Church of Ireland, argues that both the materialist view of the universe (only material entities exist) and the dualist view of the universe (there are mental and material entities) lead not only to skepticism, but also to atheism. After all, a universe that can run without God can surely dispense with him.

By eliminating the distinction between the mind and material objects, Berkeley thinks he can guarantee the reality of our ideas:

> The table I write on, I say, exists, that is, I see and feel it; and if I were out of my study I should say it existed, meaning thereby that if I was in my study I might perceive it, or that some other perceiver actually does perceive it. (*Principles of Human Knowledge*, p. 24)

If the food you eat is spicy, but the same food tastes mild to your friend, then the spiciness is not in the food. Similarly, if Elliot sees Mr. Robot, but Angela and Darlene do not, how do we know who's correct? How do we have an accurate picture of the food, particularly if we cannot appeal to the notion that there are qualities inherent in objects external to us, qualities that produce ideas by way of our sensory apparatus, like eyes and ears?

One answer is that, since ideas are mind-dependent entities, and we perceive only our ideas, there won't be any aspect of an object that goes by unnoticed. We have, as it were, a complete picture of an object. Still, this is somewhat unsatisfactory. If Elliot perceives Mr. Robot, but no one else in the room does, we are inclined to say that Elliot's perception is flawed. Yet according to Berkeley's view, it might appear that the imaginary is no different from the real.

Not so, Berkeley tells us. To understand the distinction between the real and unreal, consider what causes our ideas. Berkeley holds that ideas are passive; perceivers do not control sensory ideas. Instead, they come to us unbidden. Ideas and perceivers who have ideas cannot, then, be the causes of sensory ideas. There must, then, be some other cause. Berkeley thinks the cause is God. It is God that sustains all possible perceptions. We can say, then, that what is independent of our control is real, at least to the extent that we haven't created it. This doesn't solve the problem of hallucinations, however, since these are not ostensibly within our control. Elliot doesn't invite Mr. Robot to appear.

Reality from Consistency

There is another consideration—the consistency of our perceptions. We don't believe for a moment that the farcical sitcom version of Elliot's life in "eps2.4_m4ster-s1ave.aes," is "real life." (Like the other episode titles, this one offers us layers of meaning. Here, we can wonder, among other things, who is the "master" of Elliot's mind.) From the campy music to the laugh tracks and green screen driving, very little about the episode fits with our ordinary perceptions—or perhaps our ordinary perceptions have been warped. Tyrell spends the episode in the back of the family car as the Aldersons take their annual family road trip. Mrs. Alderson repeatedly punches Darlene into unconsciousness. At one point, Alf, the puppet alien from the 1980s sitcom of the same name appears and runs Gideon over with the car. Later, Mr. Robot beats Tyrell, who has been kept tied up in the trunk. Even Elliot has a hard time believing everything that happens.

This might quell some of our worries about the correctness of Elliot's perceptions. After all, there is no reliable indicator of errors in perception. There is no answer key against which to evaluate the correctness of ideas. Consequently, Elliot can't be wrong about his perceptions, so when they are not orderly, consistent, vivid, and distinct, he can't detect a problem.

The regularity of our perceptions is one indication that they're real. Consider, for example, the way we experience our day: the sun always appears on the horizon at daybreak, and at various points in the sky until dusk, when another point on the horizon swallows it up. We wake to expect we will be where we were when we went to sleep the night before—we expect, in essence, that things are in order. This uniformity and regularity of our perceptions leads us to notice discrepancies, as when we have a particularly vivid dream. We wake up in an emotionally wrought state—everything seemed so real—but then we recognize where we are, what we were doing before we fell asleep, and so on. We recognize that the dream was an anomaly.

Elliot's interactions with Mr. Robot in Season 1.0 often occur in the presence of characters who do not offer Elliot or the viewer any reason to think he isn't there. Indeed, there are scenes in Season 1.0 in which Mr. Robot and Darlene are engaged in heated debates about the Dark Army, in which Mr. Robot has one-on-one conversations with Romero and Tyrell, and in which Mr. Robot bumps into a diner in the café outside Steel Mountain. Elliot has no perceptual indication—except maybe in hindsight—that Mr. Robot, or anyone else, for the matter, is a hallucination. We, Elliot's "friend," don't have any such indication, either.

Even after Elliot learns of and actively works against these illusions, his *perceptual* apparatus remains intact. So also, then, do his empirically derived ideas. It is not until Elliot has evidence that some of his perceptions are inconsistent, and so problematic—such as video showing him falling off the pier's railing ("eps1.9_zer0-day.avi")—not Mr. Robot pushing him, that his confidence falls apart.

The Check of Memory

What does give him pause from the outset of the series is his memory. More specifically, he appears to suffer from dissociative amnesia. He experiences gaps, the most severe of which involve his past. He doesn't recognize Mr. Robot as his father or Darlene as his sister. He wakes up in Tyrell's SUV with no memory of what happened. As a result, his ability to form judgments about what is true and make decisions about what action to take are severely hampered.

While Elliot may not be in error about his immediate perception that there is a man standing before him wearing a jacket with a Mr. Robot logo on it, he can, according to Berkeley, draw an erroneous inference from it, namely that the man is the mastermind of the Evil Corp hack. As Berkeley tells us, you're not mistaken about the ideas you perceive, but you can be mistaken about the inferences you make from those perceptions. For example, if you perceive an oar in water you will perceive it to be crooked. But, Berkeley says, if you think the oar will look crooked when it comes out of the water, you'll be making a mistake.

In "wh1ter0se.m4v," Elliot and Darlene sit on the boardwalk discussing the immanent collapse of Evil Corp. She's elated when he tells her that the Steel Mountain plan is set to go off in less than forty-eight hours, and tells Elliot that she loves him. "You are the best person I know," she says. He leans in and kisses her, only to be shoved away. Darlene is horrified. "Did you forget again? Did you forget who I am? I need you to tell me who you think I am." He doesn't know. He can't remember. Then it hits him. "You're my sister."

Return of the Lost

This realization sets off an avalanche of overwhelming memories. As he rides home on the subway, he asks his imaginary friend, "Were you in on this the whole time?" Then he looks into the camera and yells, "Were you?!" If we perceive what Elliot does, it seems unlikely. In retrospect, however, the signs were there.

Back at home, Elliot hacks himself, but there is no online footprint of his existence. "I'm a ghost." It's only when he looks through his archive of previous hacks that he finds a disc with photos of Mr. Robot, whom he realizes is his father. What he doesn't know yet—what we don't know, yet, but might suspect—is that his father is dead.

In the next episode ("eps1.8_m1rr0r1ng.qt") we're introduced to other perspectives on Elliot's experiences, which press the issue of perceptual consistency. In a climactic scene, Mr. Robot brings a wounded and emotionally distraught Elliot to a grave. In the distance, we can hear Darlene and Angela calling out. Mr. Robot implores him to remain loyal, as if the two women are the enemy. As Elliot grows even more agitated, Mr. Robot declares, "They're going to try to get rid of me again . . . I will never leave you alone again."

When Darlene and Angela catch up, Elliot demands to know what's happening—and then he realizes where he is. "This can't be happening," he says to us repeatedly. "This is happening, isn't it? You knew all along, didn't you?"

Angela asks gently, "Elliot, who do you think you've been talking to?"

"You're going to make me say it, aren't you?" he asks us. "I am Mr. Robot."

Is he? Perhaps. Once we think we've gotten to the bottom of the perceptual rabbit hole, however, a new one is dug at the beginning of Season 2.0. Elliot maintains a rigorous routine to keep Mr. Robot at bay, to keep his perceptions consistent. The only problem, we learn, is it isn't real ("h4ndshake.sme"). Curiously enough, Elliot has known all along. "I'd like it if we could trust each other again," he tells us. Recall at the end of Season 1.0, Elliot was mad at us, his "friend." He thought we were in on a plot to deceive him about Mr. Robot's identity.

But if trust is based on sense perception, we already knew at the end of Season 2.0 we were in for more trouble in Season 3.0.

18
Psycho-Politics in a Burnout Society

FERNANDO GABRIEL PAGNONI BERNS
AND EMILIANO AGUILAR

The pilot episode of *Mr. Robot* begins with Elliot Alderson talking with someone through first-person voiceover. At first, it seems that our main hero is talking to us, the audience. The episode is aptly titled "eps1.0_hellofriend.mov." Cool, right?

Soon enough, however, we understand that he's talking to himself, or at least, to some imaginary friend that he has created in his mind—someone to talk candidly to, since he is so uncomfortable talking to others. He really needs a friendly person to speak to so he can remain sane through the show, exhausted as he is.

As a hacker, maybe the best out there, his job is being connected 24/7. He passes more time in cyberspace than with real people. And when Elliot is in the real world, he sees people in "virtual" terms, as online profiles ("eps1.6_v1ew-s0urce.flv"). Elliot's only way to remain sane within this context is through consumption of drugs, which prevents him from falling into a state of total depression.

In this sense, *Mr. Robot* illustrates the new "burnout society" immersed into *psycho-politics* as defined by the Korean-German philosopher Byung-Chul Han. The term refers to the way in which we, the "users," participate in our own exploitation, by willingly giving our personal lives to the corporate internet. We must all be *transparent* in the sense of living and being exposed online.

On the other hand, Malek's performance as a young man constantly in a numb state embodies to perfection the new society of fatigue: his attention deficits, social anxiety disorder, and depression capture our current "burnout society."

You Are So Vulnerable in the Transparent Society

In "eps1.3_da3m0ns.mp4," someone mentions the possibility of a creator taking all the hacker culture and turning it into a TV show (into something called *Mr. Robot*, perhaps?). But what would a "hacker culture" be? Probably one in which everyone speaks in jargon and lives connected in cyberspace. It would also be a culture in which citizens are extremely vulnerable. This vulnerability emerges from the fact that, unlike in previous decades, people have become "transparent." People insert themselves within the "smooth streams of capital, communication, and informationsputs it (*The Transparency Society*, p. 1). All the information of our lives is stacked in cyberspace. Further, our inner feelings (sadness, joy, desire to get romantically involved with someone, and so forth) also reside within the bowels of the virtual world. Our state of mind is open for everyone (or at least, for friends and acquaintances) on Facebook ("I'm so sad because . . ."), Twitter ("I hate you . . .") or chats ("I'm so hot!"). For lazy people, there are even little figures that encapsulate our feelings: they're called "emoticons," a blend of "emotion" and "icons," precisely because they work as brief sketches or condensations of our emotional state. With the use of emoticons, we diminish ourselves. We become transparent since our interiority, the only thing sacred, is open for everyone to see.

This predicament described by Han is perfectly illustrated in the relationship that Elliott shares with his psychologist, Krista Gordon. They both try to interpret each other's inner self. Elliot attends Krista's sessions because he's obliged to do so. He feels true sympathy towards her: she is a "good woman" with "good intentions." Psychology is a form of intimacy, a formula for transparency, according to Han, since it extracts from the deep.

According to Elliot, however, Krista "is really bad at reading people." Krista tries to get deep into her patient's psyche, but it is Elliot who truly has the upper hand in the game of "knowing each other." Elliot mostly lies to Krista (at least, until he apparently opens up to her in "eps1.6_v1ews0urce.flv"). He is opaque to her, no matter which psychoanalytic tool she uses on him. On the other hand, she is truly transparent to Elliot since he has been hacking her from day one. Her password is her favorite singer (Dylan) and her birthday backwards. Two intimate facts that are hacked just because she has been stacking her life into the internet. As time goes by, Krista is no closer to understanding Elliot, while he knows her in an intimate way. It's almost as if, in today's society, people's subconscious selves lie within the abyss of the internet.

Our immersions within the bowels of the virtual world run parallel to our immersion within capitalism. When we deposit ourselves within a machine, we become a functional element within the system of capitalism. Facebook is there to make money, folks. It is a good channel to express yourself, but the ultimate goal of social media is to make money, so when you click to login into a platform, you are accessing and accepting capitalism. Yes, even if you log in to protest against capitalism through your account on Twitter or your own blog. Just accept it.

In the show's pilot, Elliot reflects on all this: we are our property, our money, all the things we buy because someone says we need to. We become zeroes and ones, just numbers once we log into cyberspace, our intimacy, our inner self rendered transparent. This is what Han calls "the violence of transparency." The imperative of transparency eliminates any safe refuge for the individual. Transparency is an effect of the economic process, a neoliberal device that converts all life into data.

Non-transparency is an intrinsically human characteristic. People need some space for privacy, but our current society asks for a complete abandonment of the private sphere to embrace, in turn, transparency. Denying this transparency can be seen as a form of "negativity." By making things translucent, transparency produces sameness. Transparent things are deprived of all "negativity", that is ambiguity or opaqueness. For Han, resistance to transparency is intrinsically "negative." A society, which is deprived of all "negativity" becomes a "positive society." By eliminating ambiguity while favoring sameness, the "positive society" accelerates the economic system.

For Elliot, it's good that people are transparent, easily readable: that gives him power over strangers. In turn, he prefers to remain opaque or "negative" to anybody, keeping his real feelings in the dark. He lies to Krista and keeps Angela's boyfriend Ollie tiptoeing around him. Ollie cannot pin down Elliot. In a transparency society, Elliot's impermeability gives him an advantage because while he keeps his privacy intact, all the others are easy to read and as such, to violate. Hackers take advantage of people's transparency while they, for the most part, remain inaccessible to others.

There is still surface, of course. People on the internet favor fakeness. Transparency and truth are not identical. After all, we mostly put masks on our faces when coming outside, to the (virtual) world. When Elliot hacks Tyrell Wellick, he finds only a perfect life: pretty wife, smiles, all clean and proper ("eps1.1_ones-and-zer0es.mpeg"). Elliot, rightly, comes to the conclusion that all this is just surface. Wellick knows he will be hacked. There is more, however, deep down. Wellick must be made transparent, that's all.

The transparency society has no color, no ideology. Traditional politics are just spectacle rather than truth, opinions rather than ideas (*The Transparency Society*, p. 7). Opinions have no consequence, while ideology survives—hence the importance of the revolution that fsociety proposes. Together, they can terminate current politics, saturated with capitalism and emptied of real ideology.

In "eps1.7_wh1ter0se.m4v," Darlene wakes up with some occasional lover, a yuppie-type. She is looking at the skyscrapers, wondering about what would happen if money just disappeared from the face of the world. He quickly states that it is too early for ideology, but Darlene has made her statement (the one that she shares with Mr. Robot): there is no more ideology, but just rich and poor, both of them willing to give up their freedoms to corporations. Welcome to psycho-politics.

Mind Asleep, Body Awake

When surfing the Internet we feel free, stripped of psychic and physical identity when adopting new roles on condition of anonymity. It is this sense of freedom, warns Byung-Chul Han, that creates a new technique of domination, which he calls psycho-politics—the exercise of control over individuals by unconsciously directing their interests. Unlike the ancient techniques of power and domination exercized by the older ruling classes, based on punishment and repression, direct control of what individuals do, psycho-politics moves away from punishment, to give way to seduction. There are now therapies teaching us how to beat our addiction to computers and cell phones.

In the midst of a process of detoxification to weaken the influence of Mr. Robot in "eps2.0_unm4sk-pt1.tc," Elliot repeatedly writes in his journal "I am in control." Cut off from the virtual world and, above all, ignoring the presence and voice of Mr. Robot (his other self), Elliot tries to take control of his actions and thoughts. But all control, the series tell us, is a mere illusion. Byung-Chul Han points out that the subject, who is believed to be freed from external constraints and coercion from others, is not truly free, but rather subjected to internal coercion in terms of performance and optimization. Thus, Elliot's belief in self-control and in the possibility of escape from the circle of domination vanishes ("eps2.2_init_1.asec"): as long as the system remains standing, complete freedom is impossible. We have the system incorporated in our flesh and mind: hence, what Han calls psycho-politics.

Elliot seeks to circumvent his schizophrenia by integrating himself into the system. Still, the disconformity buried within him obliges Elliot to reconcile with his other self, Mr. Robot, and with what he does best: hack the system.

Han wonders whether we want to be really free. According to Han, we invented God so that we could avoid being free. Then the figure of God becomes capital, whose operation puts us in perpetual indebtedness: this indebtedness prevents us from having freedom of action, and, therefore, shows us that capitalist freedom is a delusion. Elliot defines religions ("eps2.1_k3rnel-pan1c.ksd") as "exclusive groups created to manage control" and compares a dealer with a leader whose followers are addicted to the "dopamine of ignorance." Elliot claims that "all religions are metastasizing mind worms meant to divide us, so it is easier to rule us." Religious faith would only lead down the path of subordination.

Han also speaks of delusion when referring to the digital network: while it offers unlimited freedom, there is only total control and vigilance. Elliot, hacking the data of all the people with whom he relates, is, in some way, working as a panoptic center from which he controls the lives of those around him. But he is not the only one. As the series develops, control "from above" is heavily felt: business control (Season 1.0) or government (with a ubiquitous FBI in Season 2.0).

According to Han, this digital panopticon (an institutional building that allows all inmates to be observed by a single watchman who remains invisible to the inmates) is even more efficient than the disciplinary panopticon of old, because it works in the opposite way: far from isolation, the "resident" inmates actively participate in the building of the system, giving up their freedom willingly.

This is the great trap constructed by the digital network: not only are we not free at a micro level (being prey, for example to mobile devices that isolate us from people while we are preoccupied with hunting Pokemons), but at the macro levels: corporations and governments which have control of our life data.

This is easy to see in "eps2.6_succ3ss0r.p12." fsociety hacked the secret of Operation Berenstain, an illegal FBI surveillance initiative executed in conjunction with twenty-two brand-name tech companies, violating the privacy of three million Americans. The presence of Minister Zhang, Chinese Head of State Security, adds another layer to the system of surveillance: he's an invisible power who spies on those who spy. Everyone is under surveillance and just a cog within the mechanics of the great System.

The coercion of the system is hidden behind its apparent inoffensiveness. After being kidnapped, Angela is interrogated by a girl in a dimly lit room ("eps2.9_pyth0n-pt1.p7z"). Angela must answer crude questions ("Have you ever cried during sex?"; "Have you ever fantasized about murdering your father?") mixed with others more absurd or basic, only to arrive at an ambiguous but decisive question: is the key in the room? This is how the capitalist system operates: in the face of too much information, we tend to overlook the uselessness of most of it, and we consume absolutely everything that the virtual media regurgitates. Angela, like us, keeps answering the demands of the system, integrated as she is into the psycho-politics.

This over-saturation with essentially nothing is a typical symptom of the burnout society, where we just keep filling our brains with white noise while pushing ourselves to the limit, as Elliot does.

Saturated with Nothing

Following Han, the modern subjects believe themselves to be free. However, even time for leisure is channeled into a cultural industry, which is mechanized and aimed at making life under capitalism tolerable. Thus, we are reaching a point of exhaustion through "neuronal violence," understood as excessive thinking, saturation of information and connectivity to social media.

With this movement to hyper-connectivity and excess of mental work, new forms of illness have come to replace the old bacterial diseases. So, stress, panic attacks, phobias, attention deficit, borderline personalities, are here to stay. These are the new ailments of our current age.

In *Mr. Robot*, this new era is embodied in many characters, Elliot being the perfect example. From the first episode Elliot's many mental issues are clearly laid out. His speech with an imaginary friend opens the series; he endures many fits of crying without any clear reason other than sense of "loneliness," and he has a short attention span. As a man continuously connected to the internet, he is used to websites, pop ups, decode number series and zapping in general. In "eps1.0_hellofriend.mov," Krista must bring Elliot back from his lapses of attention. In the same episode, Angela chastises Elliot because Elliot's mind is elsewhere while she's speaking to him. Elliot suffers from depression, deficits of attention, delusions and paranoia. He is the perfect embodiment of our burnout society.

He is, however, not the only one. To a lesser extent, other characters find it difficult to control their burnout. Gideon, Elliot's boss at Allsafe, is a little nervous man constantly in a state of anxiety about the future of the company. He seems to live in chronic fatigue, always tired and close to the point of throwing in the towel. More interesting is the case of Tyrell Wellick. In the first episodes, he seems to be Elliot's opposite: Wellick is astute, sure of himself and a man who embraces capitalism with gusto.

As the episodes go by, however, Tyrell comes closer to Elliot: Tyrell begins to break apart and show his true colors as a man on the brink of a nervous breakdown. In "eps1.6_v1ews0urce.flv," Tyrell strangles and kills Sharon Knowles, the wife of his enemy. He does so not in cold blood, but through a fit of uncontrollable rage and mental collapse. Immediately after killing her, he is depicted as a man in a state of panic who does not know what to do next, his prior demeanor of coldness crumbles. In "eps1.7_wh1ter0se.m4v," the camera shoots Tyrell's face in extreme focus with everything else around him blurred, so audiences must concentrate on his face: the face of a burned out man. Tyrell screams, laughs, and almost cries all in one short scene, highlighting his state as a businessman close to mental breakdown.

He needs headphones and loud music to get through the day, as a way of separating himself from the harshness of his exhausting life. Meanwhile, his wife Joanna verges on hysteria when trying to get her dress clean. We must keep in mind that the Wellicks are *villains*, the ones who should be doing some evil plotting and scheming, not constantly at the verge of tears. And this is one of the main points of the show, and one that perfectly illustrates Han's burnout society: everyone works hard to achieve success, but all the characters only arrive at more mental exhaustion. They all live with the violence of positivity: they must be more effective, more communicative and more productive all the time.

In "eps1.7_wh1ter0se.m4v," Elliot speaks with Whiterose, the mysterious hacker whom fsociety tried multiple times to meet. She clearly states that Elliot has just three minutes, so he must measure correctly his time and maximize its usefulness by asking the right questions, a perfect illustration of a society asking us to use every second to make advancements, and "useful" things without distractions. Lack of concentration is total failure, as Whiterose says. "There are always deadlines, there are always ticking clocks. That's why you must manage your time."

This new burnout era has consequences, one of the most important, the need for "helpers" to get through the day. Elliot needs drugs and the help of a psychologist to survive his mental fatigue. Both Krista and Shayla run away from their loneliness by dating horrible men. Gideon, in turns, is extremely dependent on Elliot, the best hacker in the world. Gideon knows that his company survives economically because he's lucky enough to have Elliot as an employee. Tyrell escapes from reality through music, booze and mental instability. Ollie runs away from his stress though illicit love affairs. Everyone needs crutches to walk. This "fatigue of the materials" made them weak and dependent.

But mostly, people depend on technology to fix all their problems, even those invented by technology itself. Our dependence on technology makes us weak and vulnerable to external attacks. There's no more distinction between the outside and the self, because we breathe technology. Hackers use E Corp general counsel Susan Jacobs's highly technologized house against her to force her out for some days ("eps2.0_unm4sk-pt1.tc"). Our possessions have taken possession of us. In fact, Susan's house seems diabolically possessed, with a life of its own. Our technology is more alive than we are.

Real Life Out There

In the Season 2.0 finale, Tyrell is terrified of not knowing what will become of him, given the uncertainty of the system's instability. The roller coaster and the blackened sky speak for Elliot, who doubts himself and his actions. But he must move on. He senses the main internal contradiction since his underground group works as the transparency society does: through systemic coercion. Therein lies the main problem of the neoliberal system, for those who want to understand it. Like Elliot, you cannot be sure of anything: everything is suspect and it is difficult to discriminate real freedom from fakery.

Still, there is some hope. In the first episode of Season 2.0, when Elliot hacks the entire system, Tyrell claims that it feels like "the entire world coming alive." It seems there is real life out there. But it lies outside the system and the leisure time created by it. And so, as this chapter comes to a close, go outside and let some sunshine and fresh air fall on your face.

19
Please Tell Me You're Seeing This Too

Verena Ehrnberger

Somehow Mr. Robot managed to install itself onto our hard drives, to debug our societal mindset, and give us some tools to develop a new take on the world that surrounds us. All without us really noticing. Just like a Trojan horse. All we have to do is to hit execute . . . But let's reboot for a second and take a closer look.

Mr. Robot is all about the questions it raises. While the question "Who is Mr. Robot?" might already have been answered, many more important questions remain. Let's try to answer these two:

1. **How did Mr. Robot manage to hook us so easily?** And,

2. **Why did Mr. Robot hook us in the first place?**

Install: How Mr. Robot Got Us Hooked

"Even I am not crazy enough to believe that distortion of reality."

For a Trojan horse to work, it has to be intriguing. Elliot loves reading people. He hacks into their computers, into their brains, into their lives. But when it comes to Elliot, we're not that lucky. As his friends (at least that is how he addresses us right from the start) we would love to get to know him, of course. The thing is, he isn't making it very easy for us.

Elliot starts off by telling us about some men in black who are following him. Then, we find out that he's seeing a therapist, and that he's on meds because of his delusions. Shortly after that, we find out about his drug problem. Right from the start, our trust in Elliot's account of the story rests on shaky ground. This puts us into a position where we have to decide if all of this is real or imaginary. Like when Darlene and Angela meet for ballet class: This is one of the moments where we realize that something has to be wrong with Elliot's perception of reality. But we still can't quite figure out what, exactly.

Narrative techniques like this belong to a literary genre called "the fantastic." Some describe fantastic storytelling as a conflict between reality and possibility, some describe it as a crack in the real world. In fantastic storytelling, we sense that there's something wrong with the world we perceive, but we can't quite make out what. That's what philosopher and literary critic Tzvetan Todorov calls the "ambiguity of the fantastic." We try to distinguish between what is real and what is imaginary, but we can't ever decide with absolute certainty.

As Elliot's friends we're torn between his perspective on the world and the outer perspective that his therapist Krista represents. Every time we're convinced that this must all be in Elliot's head, we nevertheless can't help thinking: *Well, is it though?* As Todorov explains: "The fantastic belongs to this moment of uncertainty." Elliot's insanity becomes more and more apparent throughout the story. But his unreliability is exactly what makes him such an intriguing narrator, who makes us want to watch and rewatch the show over and over again. The beauty of fantastic literature, is that—even when you reach that part of the story where the ambiguity is gone—you can still rewatch it, because you're watching an entirely different story the second time around.

Initially we believe in the narrative or story that Elliot appears to believe in: A lonely tech guy who gets slowly sucked into the elaborate plan of a madman who wants to overthrow the world order as we know it. We also perceive the other characters as Elliot does. Darlene, for example, seems rude and crazy, because she's not treating Elliot very nicely when she first meets him, and she seems to have no boundaries at all, like when she breaks into his apartment to take a shower. When Elliot confronts Mr. Robot with Darlene's rude behavior, he simply says "Yeah, that's Darlene." This implies that she's always like that, which leads us to perceive Darlene as a ruder character than she actually is.

After finding out about the true identity of Mr. Robot, we see an entirely different story: A schizophrenic hacker mastermind who is not at all the innocent bystander that Elliot wants us to believe. The story changes. And so does our perception of the characters.

Knowing that Darlene and Elliot are related to each other makes Darlene not seem that rude and crazy anymore, but rather like a sister who's annoyed by her brother's weird behavior towards her. She doesn't know yet that Elliot's brain has reset itself, and that he is convinced that he's meeting her for the very first time.

Even after we already know that Elliot will never tell us everything about what's going on (because he doesn't know either), we still have to believe him to some degree. Because Elliot is the one telling us this story. So, every season we find ourselves asking the same question again: *Is this really happening?* We're forced to wonder about Elliot's prison-like new routine, about Angela's intentions at E Corp and whether Tyrell is dead or alive. At least in the beginning of Season 2.0 Elliot is reminding us of his unreliability: "I'm not ready to trust you yet, not after what you did. You kept things from me, and I don't know if I can tell you secrets like before." So, when we finally find out about all the things Elliot has not been revealing to us, we shouldn't be surprised. But, we are. And that's exactly the charm of the fantastic.

Fantastic storytelling almost forces us to watch it all over again to find those little moments in the story where we could have worked it out, and where we admire the subtlety with which the authors introduced lots of hints, but without ever really pointing us towards the solution. In fantastic storytelling there's not just one story being told; there are many. And we have to work through the different layers of illusion to get to the truth. But how can we ever really work out the truth, if our narrator Elliot is that unreliable? Everything could be an illusion. The whole story—AllSafe, E Corp, Tyrell, and Angela—could all be a crazy drug-induced dream. Elliot might not even be awake . . . But does it really matter what's real and what's not? Fantastic storytelling is how Mr. Robot got us hooked. So, now it's time to focus on the Why.

Exploit: The Filter of the Culture Industry

"I could be a Trojan horse."

Right in the beginning, Elliot reveals to us what bugs him about society: "The world itself is just one big hoax. Spamming each other with our burning commentary of bullshit masquerading as insight, our social media faking as intimacy."

Elliot longs for a life in this "bubble," in "the reality of the naive," as he calls it. He wants to protect the optimism of the people who are lucky enough not to know that their cozy reality is an illusion. At the same time, Mr. Robot wants to take down exactly this cozy illusionary world. Elliot's memorable monologue about society also contains a critique of the industry Mr Robot, in fact, belongs to: the "culture industry." "We all know why we do this, not because *The Hunger Games* books make us happy, but because we wanna be sedated. Because it's painful not to pretend, because we're cowards." Isn't it a paradox that Mr. Robot keeps criticizing the industry it belongs to? But that's the thing about Trojan horses: They hide within seemingly harmless programs.

Critical theorist Theodor W. Adorno lived in a time when consumerism and conglomerates where not the norm yet; but at the end of World War II he saw this society coming, and warned us about it—the society we live in today, every day. Culture in our modern times has become nothing more than an industry. Its goal is to make money and to distract the people from their monotonous daily routines and their dull work life. The culture industry's function is to sedate us, so that we accept the fate modern society has thought up for us: the mind-numbing sameness of work. Or in Adorno's words: "The consumers are the workers and salaried employees, the farmers and petty bourgeois. Capitalist production hems them in so tightly, in body and soul, that they unresistingly succumb to whatever is proffered to them."

For Adorno, the culture industry was a tool of mass deception. He observed how books, radio shows, and movies were used for the "idolization of the existing order." All these goods produced by the culture industry only had one goal: to feed the masses fantasies they could believe in, so that they would not question the societal structures they were born into.

"The defrauded masses today," Adorno writes, "cling to the myth of success still more ardently than the successful. They insist unwaveringly on the ideology by which they are enslaved." The culture industry was the perfect way to propagate those myths. Believing in freedom of choice and in a system that will reward our achievements is far less upsetting than acknowledging the status quo. Since Adorno's times the culture industry has changed a lot. Today, there's not only a market for love stories and action movies, there's also a market for nonconformist shows like *Mr. Robot*.

With regard to the culture industry, Adorno was convinced that "anyone who resists can survive only by being incorporated." It does not matter how good a book, a movie, or any other cultural good is, we will only get to see it if it is passed through "the filter of the culture industry" first. Every cultural good has to find its distributor. Only the culture industry is able to reach mass audiences. Which is why it is such an ideal tool for the idolization of the current system in power. But it can also be used for other purposes. So, might it be that Mr. Robot also uses the culture industry as a tool? As FBI Agent Dom DiPierro notes: "They are hackers. Brazen. They believe in hiding in plain sight."

Debug: An Unmasked World

"That's just how they own you."

Once a Trojan horse has been social-engineered into our system, it executes at frequent intervals when we turn on our computer. (Just like, let's say, a TV show.) When we enter Elliot's weird, insane, and paranoid world, we're forced to question our own world too: *Who are we? Is this really happening to us? Please tell me you are seeing this too . . .*

Is the status quo we believe in even a reliable narration? Don't we oftentimes sense those little cracks in the continuity of our everyday narrative that make us suspicious that something might be wrong with our reality? So, the point might not be that Elliot questions the world he lives in. The whole point might be that we, just like him, start doing it too. As Mr. Robot says: "You are here because you sense something wrong with the world. Something you can't explain. But you know it controls you and everyone you care about."

Mr. Robot implies that the world we live in is not real, that we too (like Elliot) believe in illusions that imprison us. But no need to worry about that—Mr. Robot already has a plan to save us: "We are on the verge of taking down this virtual reality." The idea of debugging reality is not new. Tyler Durden had it. And Neo too was about liberating the people from their mental prisons. Mr. Robot raises this old question again, that maybe the status quo is not the best solution there is for us human beings. Debugging, as we know, is all about finding the bug, and about understanding why it was there to begin with. So, let's try to get a good look at the bug.

Today, we live in an enlightened world. Enlightenment basically means that we're convinced that we've unmasked all the myths humanity ever believed in—like magic, fate, or even God. "Enlightenment, understood in the widest sense as the advance of thought, has always aimed at liberating human beings from fear and installing them as masters," Adorno explains. Enlightenment means an intellectual understanding that enables us to perceive reality as it really is.

We have scientifically measured and explained the world that surrounds us. And we're pretty proud of it too. We don't believe in the silly myths and superstitions that controlled the people of past times. "Enlightenment's program was the disenchantment of the world," Adorno reminds us. "It wanted to dispel myths, to overthrow fantasy with knowledge." Today, we're convinced that we have reached this goal. We're convinced that we know everything there is to know about the world. But is this really the case?

We are born into the paradigms of our time, and we rarely question them. Many people live with the paradigms they were taught to believe in, without ever suspecting that there might be a world beyond their perception of reality. There have been many default settings in the course of history: feudality (where the people were generating profits for their earthly lords), churches (where the people were generating profits for their heavenly lords), or nationalism (where the people were generating profits for their states). At least, the people of past times knew whom they were generating profits for. Today, all our earnings go directly into the economy. Our "corporate overlords" have become faceless. Anonymous. Adorno was sure that there can't be freedom in society without enlightened thinking, but he was also convinced that enlightenment is not only good for us. It does have its negative effects too. If we do not acknowledge those negative effects, we risk falling for modern mythologies while firmly believing that we are in control of our lives. As Adorno says, "False clarity is only another name for myth."

By trying to abolish superstition and myths, enlightenment ignored its own mythical aspects. In Adorno's view, enlightenment only poses as a "myth-free," and therefore superior, view on the world. The myth of the mythlessness of our world is what controls us today. Our world is still full of myths. We just don't believe in their existence anymore. But if we take a good look at the world Elliot is showing us, this world is full of modern mythologies: meritocracy's fairy tale of achievement as the ultimate goal, consumerism as a way to happiness, and digitalisation as a means to conquer loneliness. That's what Adorno means when he writes "Myth is already enlightenment, and enlightenment reverts to mythology." Or: "Meritocracy, my ass," as Darlene puts it.

Develop: The Inevitable Upgrade of Society

"The bug forces the software to adapt, evolving into something new because of it."

Mr. Robot managed to pull off the hack of the century. But, what happens when all the data is corrupted after an attack? Elliot and Darlene want to free the people from the modern mythologies they live in. But this upgrade of society has its pitfalls.

In 1944, Adorno took it upon himself to examine the negative effects of enlightenment, together with his colleague Max Horkheimer: "What we had set out to do was nothing less than to explain why humanity, instead of entering a truly human state, is sinking into a new kind of barbarism." Enlightenment, as we already know, is a double-edged sword. And freedom isn't any different. We need freedom to live a truly fulfilled life. But not everybody is able to handle the responsibility that comes with it.

Elliot's romantic notion to free the masses is understandable. But everything comes at a price, even freedom. The price of freedom is responsibility. If we are free, we decide for ourselves. We rely on ourselves, and ourselves alone. There's no one to lean on, no one to ask, if we ever feel unsure. Freedom doesn't only mean the chance of personal fulfilment. It also means being the sole person responsible for this fulfilment. For people who have difficulty taking on responsibility, this can seem like a burden. In addition, freedom makes it possible to take action and therefore also to fail. Potentially failing is scary. So, freedom can be a pretty scary concept.

Freedom might be a desirable goal for people who are confident enough to handle that responsibility. But what about those who can't? What about the Kristas and Ollies of the world who enjoy the bubble they live in? The sociologist Alain Ehrenberg, famous for his study of the modern epidemic of depression, theorizes that there might even be a correlation between those expectations of autonomy and the rise of depression in our society. Today, we are all expected to be autonomous. But, some people are just not the autonomous type—either because they prefer to have a system of rules to guide them or because they have simply never learned how to rely on themselves. Ehrenberg observed that depression began to rise when the rules of authority that gave social classes a specific destiny were traded for norms that expected us to take personal initiative and be ourselves. That's why he calls depression the "illness of responsibility": "The depressed individual is unable to measure up; he is tired of having to become himself."

Enlightenment "already contains the germ of the regression," Adorno writes. The reason why people voluntarily regress to modern mythologies might lie in the fact that most people fear actual freedom, because freedom equals responsibility. Modern mythologies offer a way out of this responsibility: we don't have to decide everything for ourselves. Some things are just the way they are. This way, there's always someone to blame if things go wrong. And this someone is definitely not us. The "germ of regression" might lie in this fear of a truly autonomous life. "Depression," Ehrenberg writes, "is the familiar shadow of a person without a guide, tired of going forward to achieve the self and tempted to sustain himself through products and behaviors."

Will we find our true selves again in this unmasked world, as Elliot believes? Will we pull off the mask or will we put one on? Will we change the world or will we play the game? As we know, in the end it all comes down to one essential question: *Are you a 1 or a 0?* Maybe Elliot is right: "Maybe it's not about avoiding the crash. But it's about setting a breakpoint to find the flaw in the code, fix it, and carry on until we hit the next flaw, the quest to keep going, to always fight for footing."

And to evolve into something new because of it.

Bibliography

Adorno, Theodor W. 2001. *The Culture Industry: Selected Essays on Mass Culture*. Routledge.

Aristotle. 1975. *Categories and De Interpretatione*. Oxford University Press.

———. 1999. *Nicomachean Ethics*. Hackett.

———. 2001. *The Basic Works of Aristotle*. Modern Library.

———. 2016. *Metaphysics*. Hackett.

Baudrillard, Jean. 1994. *Simulacra and Simulation*. University of Michigan Press.

Bentham, Jeremy. 2008. *Panopticon: Or, the Inspection House*. Dodo.

Berkeley, George. 1979. *Three Dialogues Between Hylas and Philonous*. Hackett.

———. 1982. *A Treatise Concerning the Principles of Human Knowledge*. Hackett.

Berkman, Alexander. 2003. *What Is Anarchism?* AK Press.

Berlin, Isaiah. 1980. *Four Essays on Liberty*. Oxford University Press.

Burke, Edmund. 1997. *Edmund Burke: Selected Writings and Speeches*. Gateway.

———. 2009. *Reflections on the Revolution in France*. Oxford University Press.

Bok, Sissela. 1989. *Secrets: On the Ethics of Concealment and Revelation*. Vintage.

———. 1999. *Lying: Moral Choice in Public and Private Life*. Vintage.

Carson, Thomas L. 2012. *Lying and Deception: Theory and Practice*. Oxford University Press.

Casson, Douglas John. 2011. *Liberating Judgment: Fanatics, Skeptics, and John Locke's Politics of Probability*. Princeton University Press.

Chisholm, Roderick M., and Thomas D. Feehan. 1977. The Intent to Deceive. *Journal of Philosophy* 74.

Chomsky, Noam. 1999. *Profit over People: Neoliberalism and Global Order*. Seven Stories.

———. 2016. *Who Rules the World?* Metropolitan.

Debord, Guy. 2014. *The Society of the Spectacle: Annotated Edition*. Bureau of Public Secrets.

Deleuze, Gilles, and Félix Guattari. 1987. *A Thousand Plateaus: Capitalism and Schizophrenia*. University of Minneosta Press.

———. 1996. *What Is Philosophy?* Columbia University Press.

——— 2009. *Anti-Oedipus: Capitalism and Schizophrenia*. Penguin

Descartes, René. 1993. *Meditations on First Philosophy*. Hackett.

Dewey, John. 2000 [1935]. *Liberalism and Social Action*. Prometheus.

The Economist. 2008. Fair Game: An Online Onslaught agaist Scientology. *The Economist* (31st January).

Ehrenberg, Alain. 2009. *The Weariness of the Self: Diagnosing the History of Depression in the Contemporary Age*. McGill-Queens University Press.

Foucault, Michel. 2012. *The History of Sexuality, Volume 1: Introduction*. Vintage.

———. 2012. *The History of Sexuality, Volume 2: The Use of Pleasure*. Vintage.

———. 2013. *Madness and Civilization: A History of Insanity in the Age of Reason*. Vintage.

French, Peter A. 1979. The Corporation as a Moral Person. *American Philosophical Quarterly* 16:3.

———. 1992. *Responsibility Matters*. University Press of Kansas.

———. 1994. *Corporate Ethics*. Wadsworth.

Gandhi, Mohandas K. 1996. *Gandhi: Selected Political Writings*. Hackett.

———. 2001. *Non-Violent Resistance (Satyagraha)*. Dover.

Gibson, William. 2003. *Burning Chrome*. HarperCollins.

Goldman, Emma. 1978. *Red Emma Speaks: Selected Writings and Speeches*. Ashgate.

———. 2008. *Emma Goldman: A Documentary History of the Americanb Years. Volume 1, Made for America, 1890–1901*. University of Illinois Press.

Graeber, David. 2001. *Toward an Anthropological Theory of Value: The False Coin of Our Own Dreams*. Palgrave.

———. 2007. *Possibilities: Essays on Hierarchy, Rebellion, and Desire*. AK Press.

———. 2009. *Direct Action: An Ethnography*. AK Press.

———. 2011. *Debt: The First 5000 Years*. Melville House.

———. 2011. *Revolutions in Reverse: Essays on Politics, Violence, Art, and Imagination*. Autonomedia.

———. 2013. *The Democracy Project: A History, a Crisis, a Movement*. Spiegel and Grau.

———. 2016. *The Utopia of Rules: On Technology, Stupidity, and the Secret Joys of Bureaucracy*. Melville House.

Greene, Richard, and Rachel Robison-Greene. 2013. *Boardwalk Empire and Philosophy: Bootleg This Book*. Open Court.

———. 2016. *Orphan Black and Philosophy: Grand Theft DNA*. Open Court.

Greenwald, Glenn. 2016. In the Democratic Echo Chamber, Inconvenient Truths are Recast as Putin Plots. *The Intercept* (October 11th).

Han, Byung-Chul. 2015. *The Burnout Society*. Stanford University Press.

———. 2015. *The Transparency Society*. Stanford University Press

———. 2017. *Psychopolitics: Neoliberalism and New Technologies of Power*. Verso.

Hanson, Robin. 2016. *The Age of Em: Work, Love, and Life when Robots Rule the Earth*. Oxford University Press.

Harvey, David. 2014. *Seventeen Contradictions and the End of Capitalism*. Oxford University Press.

Hedges, Chris. 2002. *War Is a Force that Gives Us Meaning*. PublicAffairs.

———. 2010. *Death of the Liberal Class*. Nation Books.

———. 2010. *Empire of Illusion: The End of Literacy and the Triumph of Spectacle*. Nation Books.

———. 2016. *Wages of Rebellion: The Moral Imperative of Revolt*. Nation Books.

———. 2016. *Unspeakable: On the Most Forbidden Topics in America*. Hot Books.

Hobbes, Thomas. 1982. *Leviathan*. Penguin.

Holloway, John. 2010. *Change the World without Taking Power*. Pluto.

———. 2013. *Crack Capitalism*. Pluto.

Horkheimer, Max, and Theodor W. Adorno. 2002 [1947]. *Dialectic of Enlightenment: Philosophical Fragments*. Stanford University Press.

Kant, Immanuel. 2012. *Groundwork of the Metaphysics of Morals*. Cambridge University Press.

Knabb, Ken. 1997. *Public Secrets: Collected Skirmishes of Ken Knabb*. Bureau of Public Secrets.

———. 2017. *The Joy of Revolution*. Theory and Practice.

Knei-Paz, Baruch. 1978. *The Social and Political Thought of Leon Trotsky*. Oxford University Press.

Locke, John. 1959. *An Essay Concerning Human Understanding*. Dover.

Marcuse, Herbert. 1991. *One Dimensional Man: Studies in the Ideology of Advanced Industrial Society*. Beacon.

Marshall, Peter. 2010. *Demanding the Impossible*. PM Press.

Marx, Karl H. 1992. *Early Writings*. Penguin.

———. 1994. *Selected Writings*. Hackett.

Marx, Karl H., and Friedrich Engels. 2014 [1848]. The Communist Manifesto. International.

More, Thomas. 2012 [1516]. *Utopia*. Penguin.

Morris, James McGrath. 2014. *Revolution by Murder: Emma Goldman, Alexander Berkman, and the Plot to Kill Henry Clay Frick*. Amazon (ebook).

Nielsen, Kai. 2003. *Globalization and Justice*. Humanity.

———. 2016. On the Ethics of Revolution. *Radical Philosophy*.

Nietzsche, Friedrich. 1974. *The Gay Science: With a Prelude in Rhymes and an Appendix of Songs*. Vintage.

———. 1961. *Thus Spoke Zarathustra: A Book for Everyone and No One*. Penguin.

———. 2003. *Beyond Good and Evil*. Penguin,

———. 2014. *On the Genealogy of Morals*. Penguin.

Plato. 2005. *The Collected Dialogues of Plato*. Princeton University Press.

Ralston, Shane. 2011. *John Dewey's Great Debates—Reconstructed*. Information Age.

Rousseau, Jean-Jacques. 1988. *On the Social Contract*. Hackett.

Schneider, Nathan. 2011. *Thank You Anarchy: Notes from the Occupy Apocalypse*. University of California Press.

Bibliography

Smaligo, Nicholas. 2014. *The Occupy Movement Explained: From Corporate Control to Democracy*. Open Court.

Todorov, Tzvetan. 1975. *The Fantastic: A Structural Approach to a Literary Genre*. Cornell University Press.

Trotsky, Leon, John Dewey, and George Novack. 1969. *Their Morals and Ours: Marxist versus Liberal Views on Morality*. Pathfinder.

Vaneigem, Raoul. 2012. *The Revolution of Everyday Life*. PM Press.

Velasquez, Manuel G. 1983. Why Corporations Are Not Morally Responsible for Anything They Do. *Business and Professional Ethics Journal* 2:3.

Wells, H.G. 2006. *A Modern Utopia*. Penguin.

Wolff, Richard, and David Barsamian. 2012. *Occupy the Economy: Challenging Capitalism*. City Lights.

phsociety

EMILIANO AGUILAR is a graduate student at the Universidad de Buenos Aires (UBA), Facultad de Filosofía y Letras (Argentina). He once published a chapter in *Orphan Black and Philosophy: Grand Theft DNA*. As for his co-authored chapter in this volume, Emiliano has serious doubts about its authorship. He does not remember writing it and has not recently seen his co-author and esteemed colleague, Fernando Gabriel Pagnoni Berns. In fact he has begun to doubt that Fernando really exists. Or Argentina, for that matter.

JOHN ALTMANN is an independent scholar in philosophy. He sees himself as an ally of fsociety, but seeing as how he's not tech-savvy enough to turn on his computer without help, Elliot may not be looking to recruit him anytime soon.

FERNANDO GABRIEL PAGNONI BERNS is a professor at the Universidad de Buenos Aires (UBA) (Argentina). He teaches seminars on international horror movies and has published chapters in such books as *Horrors of War: The Undead on the Battlefield*, *To See the Saw Movies: Essays on Torture Porn and Post 9/11 Horror*, and *For His Eyes Only: The Women of James Bond*. Fernando is currently masterminding an imminent massive attack on global networks, but is considering whether to upgrade from Windows 95 first.

MATTHEW WILLIAM BRAKE. Age 32. His password is "password." His secret Twitter handle is "Carlos Danger." Truth is, you shouldn't hate Matthew. He's not a bad guy. He's too insecure to be a bad guy. He has, like, three master's degrees, because of his chronic fear of failing a PhD program.

DARCI DOLL has been trying to save the world by using philosophy to plant logic bombs wherever she goes. Her goal is to program people to create virtuous if/then programming that helps them become the positive change that the world needs. These bombs can be found at Delta College and in her chapters in volumes like *The Princess Bride and Philosophy, Orphan Black and Philosophy*, and *Red Rising and Philosophy*. While she sometimes has to point out the errors in your judgment to help you find your own balance, she's always rooting for you.

VERENA EHRNBERGER studies Philosophy and Psychotherapy at the University of Vienna. Just like fsociety, she tries to save the world using tech. The only difference is: As a Data Privacy Legal Expert, she has to do it within the realms of the law. Trying to find the sweet spot in technological evolution where law and ethics meet, is one of her constant quests. (As we know, it is all about finding the bug . . .) She also blogs for TEDxVienna.

CHARLENE ELSBY is Assistant Professor and the Philosophy Program Director at Indiana University—Purdue University, Fort Wayne. She believes such designations are dependent upon the recognition of power structures that will ultimately prove meaningless.

DON FALLIS is Professor of Information and Adjunct Professor of Philosophy at the University of Arizona. He has written several philosophy articles on lying and deception, including "What is Lying?" in *The Journal of Philosophy* and "The Most Terrific Liar You Ever Saw in Your Life" in *The Catcher in the Rye and Philosophy*. Don is somewhat like Elliot in many respects, except that ur qbrf abg unir na nygre rtb jub vf gelvat gb gnxr bire gur jbeyq, ng yrnfg nf sne nf ur xabjf.

RICHARD GREENE is a Professor of Philosophy at Weber State University. He also serves as Executive Chair of the Intercollegiate Ethics Bowl. He's co-edited a number of books on pop culture and philosophy including *The Princess Bride and Philos-*

ophy, Dexter and Philosophy, Quentin Tarantino and Philosophy, Boardwalk Empire and Philosophy, and *The Sopranos and Philosophy*. Richard wishes that his dad were Mr. Robot. Alas, he's more like Mr. Roomba.

CHRISTOPHER HOYT currently teaches philosophy at Western Carolina University, but he was a software engineer in Chicago years ago and is still fascinated by technology and its social implications. He is not, we repeat, not, participating in or hoping for a revolution. Don't even suggest such a thing. In public.

TIM JONES considered using a long-winded visual metaphor over the course of several episodes to convey the generally static and sheltered nature of his life, before revealing what's actually going on in a sudden twist near the end of the season, but decided it was much simpler to just tell you directly that he's really in prison an early career academic who loves teaching but has very little interest in developing a serious research portfolio.

CHRISTOPHER KETCHAM earned his doctorate at the University of Texas at Austin. He teaches business and ethics for the University of Houston Downtown. His research interests are risk management, applied ethics, social justice, and East-West comparative philosophy. He has done recent work in the philosophical ideas of forgiveness, Emmanuel Levinas's responsibility, Gabriel Marcel's spirit of abstraction, space ethics, the ego in Buddhism and lots of chapters in Popular Culture and Philosophy volumes. Set that all aside for a moment and come closer, closer . . . good. Now listen carefully . . . Leviathan has the true alternate facts.

S. EVAN KREIDER is an associate professor of philosophy at the University of Wisconsin—Fox Valley, and holds a PhD from the University of Kansas. His research interests include ancient Greek philosophy, ethics, and aesthetics, including their applications to pop culture. In his spare time, he likes to play chess online and surf the web in incognito mode. He now realizes that he has said way too much, and should probably go scrub his computer.

ROB LUZECKY is a lecturer in philosophy at Indiana University—Purdue University, Fort Wayne. He has contributed numerous chapters to various Popular Culture and Philosophy volumes. When he is not busy planning for the coming revolution he spends his time reading and lecturing about cool thinkers like Deleuze and Ingarden.

CHRISTOPHE POROT is a graduate student and Deans Fellow recipient at Harvard University. He is managing editor, along with Dr. Charles Taliaferro, of a series on Philosophy of Religion in *Religious Studies Review*. He has also edited for *The Cambridge Companion to Platonism* and *The Stanford Encyclopedia of Philosophy*, and has multiple publications including those in the *European Journal for Philosophy of Religion*, *The Journal of Death and Anti-Death*, and volumes in the Popular Culture and Philosophy series. He is hoping to soon leave the world of philosophical reflection to enjoy the splendor of working for Evil Corp, a company he has long admired and certainly has no plans to hack from the inside in order to bring about a more just and fair society.

SHANE J. RALSTON is Associate Professor of Philosophy at Pennsylvania State University Hazleton. While he still writes academic articles, he prefers firing off controversial pieces to online issues forums such as *Truthout* and *Intellectual Takeout*. He aspires to become a hacktivist, but admits that he still can't come up with an original password or do more on a computer than edit a word processing document.

RACHEL ROBISON-GREENE is a PhD Candidate in Philosophy at UMass Amherst. She is co-editor of *The Golden Compass and Philosophy*, *Dexter and Philosophy*, *Boardwalk Empire and Philosophy*, *Girls and Philosophy*, *Orange Is the New Black and Philosophy*, and *The Princess Bride and Philosophy*. She has contributed chapters to *Quentin Tarantino and Philosophy*, *The Legend of Zelda and Philosophy*, *Zombies, Vampires, and Philosophy*, and *The Walking Dead and Philosophy*. Rachel's computer skills are limited to arguing with strangers on the internet. Or so she claims.

JAMES ROCHA is an Assistant Professor of Philosophy at Fresno State with research interests in race and racism, the criminal injustice system, and anarchism. While he wants to change the world, he finds it more comfortable to live in a world built on fantasy, where he watches stupid Marvel movies, fakes intimacy on social media, snacks on bags of GMOs, and regularly attends brainwashing seminars in the form of television shows. But, when he dreams, he dreams of using philosophy to bring about a world that's a bit more real.

HEIDI SAMUELSON is currently Visiting Assistant Professor of Philosophy at Sweet Briar College in Virginia. Although she writes and presents on the overlap of philosophy and pop culture, she, like everyone else, is merely a product of power relations perpetuated by institutional and governmental practices in a biopolitical regime. She is constantly surveilled by the panopticon, feels pressure to behave normally, and is highly suspicious of men in black suits.

MIA WOOD is Associate Professor of Philosophy at Pierce College in Woodland Hills, California, and a temporary Lecturer at the University of Rhode Island. She likes loitering at the intersection of Philosophy-and-Everything-Else, which allows her to hide out in plain sight from all those men in suits. (She's too old to look cool in a hoodie.)

Index

ORPHAN
BLACK
AND PHILOSOPHY

GRAND
THEFT DNA

Edited by
RICHARD GREENE
and **RACHEL
ROBISON-GREENE**